Abbé Prévost

ANTOINE-FRANÇOIS PRÉVOST was born in Hesdin, France, in 1697. His early education was Jesuit. In 1713 he became a novice and subsequently attended the College of La Flèche in Paris. After two brief periods of service in the army and a novitiate in the Benedictines, he took the vows of that order in 1721, and became a priest in 1726. He preached for a year at Evreux and was soon after called to Paris. In 1728, unhappy with the confinement of monastic life, Prévost left the Abbey of Saint-Germain-des-Prés without permission. Six years of exile followed in England and Holland. He devoted himself to work on a six-volume romance which he had begun at Saint-Germain-des-Prés entitled *Memoirs and Adventures of a Man of Quality* (1728-31). *Manon Lescaut* first appeared in 1731 as an appendage to *Man of Quality*. Prévost's next work was *The English Philosopher, or History of Monsieur Cleveland* (eight volumes, 1731-1739). Eager to return home and to re-enter the religious life, he was permitted to transfer to a freer Benedictine congregation by a papal brief of 1734. He was accepted into the Abbey of La Grènetière in Vendée on February 3, 1735, where he remained for the rest of his life. He died in 1763.

Manon Lescaut

ABBÉ PRÉVOST

A NEW TRANSLATION
with an introduction by
Donald M. Frame

A SIGNET CLASSIC

PUBLISHED BY THE NEW AMERICAN LIBRARY

SIGNET CLASSICS *are published by*
The New American Library of World Literature, Inc.
501 Madison Avenue, New York 22, New York

PRINTED IN THE UNITED STATES OF AMERICA

CONTENTS

Introduction by Donald M. Frame *vii*

A Note on Money Values *xv*

Story of the Chevalier des Grieux and of Manon
      Lescaut *17*

Note on the 1753 Edition *20*

Story of Manon Lescaut
      PART ONE *21*
      PART TWO 115

INTRODUCTION

Manon Lescaut is an astonishing work. Lucid, simple, compelling in its truth, it shines out against the turgid background of the sentimental, implausible prose romances of its time and country—even of its author—with the clarity of a gem. One of the great stories of fatal and ill-fated love, it has caught —in translation as well as in the original—the imagination of readers of three centuries and of many lands. It has enriched the opera, notably with three favorites composed within less than forty years of each other: the light crisp *Manon Lescaut* of Auber (1856); the tremendously popular *Manon* of Massenet (1884), poignant and sweet though rather edulcorated; and the starker *Manon Lescaut* of Puccini (1893), more faithful to Prévost's balanced picture of the weaknesses as well as the charms of the two young lovers. None of these replace the novel; they merely attest its magic. It belongs to its author's time and work, yet towers over them.

The first truly professional, self-supporting French man of letters, Prévost published a total of 113 volumes[1]—47 of translations, 66 of his own—which include histories of travel and of Dutch coinage; translations of Richardson's novels; a lively journal of literary news, *Le Pour et Contre;* various overtly moral and didactic tracts; and about thirty volumes of prose fiction, among them the *Memoirs and Adventures of a Man of Quality* (6 volumes, 1728-

[1] Henry Harrisse, *L'Abbé Prévost: Histoire de sa vie et de ses œuvres* (Paris, 1896), pp. 417-18. My total count differs from Harrisse's but is based on his list.

1731), *Manon Lescaut* (1 volume, 1731), and *The English Philosopher, or History of Monsieur Cleveland* (8 volumes, 1731-1739).

These three works are closely related. *Manon Lescaut* first appeared as an appendage to the *Man of Quality,* and *Cleveland* was Prévost's next book. All three are presented as histories and narrated in the first person. Their common themes include adventure, sentiment, pathetic deaths of beautiful heroines; fatal love that deservedly conquers all, even religious remorse; pious moralizing, often belied by the impact of the stories.

More striking are the differences that set *Manon Lescaut* apart. The two longer works are escape literature, nothing more. The *Man of Quality* has a guiding thread in the story of the narrator, who is known as Monsieur de Renoncour; but in the labyrinth of episode the reader needs—and lacks—an Ariadne. No self-respecting character fails, on his first appearance, to relate his previous adventures in full detail. Attention moves from Renoncour's father to Renoncour himself, then—since his beloved dies early and he remains faithful—to his protégé Rosemont and niece Nadine. Psychology yields to adventure, plausibility to sensation. Rosemont loses his first eternal love, Diana de Velez, stabbed by the savage mother of an abductor, but later grows alarmingly fond of the Turkish lad Memiscès. All is well, however. When the Man of Quality was a slave in Turkey, his master's son Amulem, in return for similar aid, had helped him win his sister Sélima. Memiscès is no boy but a girl in disguise, Amulem's daughter, and thus Renoncour's niece.

Cleveland, though it piles exotic adventure upon romance, has more unity through its more durable romantic hero. In a cavern in England young Cleveland, an illegitimate son of Oliver Cromwell, meets Lord Axminster and his wife, fugitives like himself from Cromwell's tyranny, tutors their lovely ten-year-old daughter Fanny, falls in love with her;

soon they will be married. However, the deposed king sends Axminster to govern his American colonies, and Cleveland is prevented from taking the same boat. As soon as he can he follows, via Martinique and Cuba, to the coast of Virginia, plunges into the interior, and at last finds the Axminsters in the woods, stripped of their clothes by savages. Presently, married to Fanny, he becomes king and lawgiver to the noble, peaceful Abaquis. Learning that Axminster is in trouble again, he goes to the rescue, sees his Abaqui warriors decimated by disease, and is captured by the fierce Rouintons, who set about cooking and eating their captives. As he and Fanny are waiting for the pot, he observes their daughter and a friend preceding them. At length the senior Clevelands are judged more valuable for barter than for consumption, and regain their freedom.

Later Fanny allows a schemer to convince her that her husband loves another woman and to escort her away from him to greater safety. Cleveland supposes she has simply deserted him. With the old love buried a new love blooms, for the beautiful Cécile. It is near consummation when Cécile summons her wits enough to speak of marriage; Cleveland admits that he has a wife. While means of annulment are under study, it is learned that Cécile is Cleveland's long-lost daughter, unroasted and uneaten after all.

Against these absurdities the story of Manon Lescaut and Des Grieux stands out by its truth and restraint. A youth and a girl fall in love, become lovers, and try to live together with little money. Craving pleasure and luxury, she repeatedly betrays and abandons him, only to return—and win him back—each time. Her money-raising devices lead to prison and finally exile to America as a prostitute. He accompanies her; she dies; he returns to virtue.

For all its pathos, the story is poignant; for all its coincidences, stark. The downfall of the lovers follows from their characters; weakness leads to misery. The reader enjoys Des Grieux's rapturous discovery of love, but soon learns with him that happiness with Manon brings betrayal, misery, and degradation. Des Grieux clings to only two values, nobiliary pride and love for Manon, but often sacrifices even the first of these to the second.

All Prévost's favorite temptations—irrelevant episode, bathos, prolixity, melodramatic psychology and coincidence—he for once stoutly resists. His story recalls the tragedies of Racine and *The Princess of Clèves* of Madame de La Fayette. He broadens their realism with his weak hero and fickle heroine, the importance of money, and the depths to which this leads them; he adds a preromantic cult of sexual love. Among the great French masters of the psychological novel, classical in its economy and intensity, he holds an honored place.

Des Grieux embodies many of Prévost's traits. His story until the trip to America is probably largely autobiographical, and certainly fits the author's life.

Unlike his heroes, Antoine-François Prévost (1697-1763) was a bourgeois, though of a family of some distinction in law, government service, and the church. He was born in Hesdin (near Calais), studied with the Jesuits at their local school (1711-1713), and went on for two years in their Novitiate in Paris. Sent to La Flèche for a course in philosophy, he soon left the school and the order to seek military glory. Disappointed by an early peace, he was again accepted into the Jesuit Novitiate, only to leave it again for another brief fling in the army, another—but unsuccessful—attempt to return to the Society. If indeed he once found and lost his own Manon, this probably happened in his early twenties and led him, after a novitiate in the Benedictines, to take (1721) the vows of that order. He was sent successively to several abbeys, then, as a teacher, to the Collège de Saint-Germer. Ordained to the priesthood in 1726, he preached for a year at Evreux and was soon after called to Paris, eventually (1728) to the Abbey of Saint-Germain-des-Prés. Al-

ready he had written much of the *Man of Quality*.
In the same year, again without permission, he left
his post. This is his explanation:

> Feeling returned to me, and I recognized that this
> all too lively heart was still burning beneath the
> ashes. The loss of my freedom distressed me to the
> point of tears. It was too late: for five or six years
> I sought consolation in the charms of study. My
> books were my faithful friends; but like myself, they
> were dead. Finally I seized the occasion of a petty
> dissatisfaction and I withdrew.[2]

His letter to his superior argues that he should
have withdrawn years before, that his superiors must
share the blame, and that he has behaved irreproach-
ably; accuses his colleagues of envious calumny;
claims that he has lost health, eyes, and repose; and
extols his character as a man of honor. He threatens
that if harshly treated he will make the Benedictines
a laughingstock, and affirms his right to leave, since
he took nothing with him. "A decent man must be
that even in trifles. You have kept me for eight
years, I have served you well; thus whatever was
owed is paid."

This escape was not received lightly. The superiors of the congregation requested the Paris police
to arrest Prévost, describing him as "a man of modest
stature, blond, large wide blue eyes, ruddy complexion, full face." To avoid certain imprisonment, he
fled the country.

His six years of exile (1728-1734) in England,
Holland, and again in England, were his most pro-
ductive. Writing was his true vocation. Free from
the constraints of the cloister, he published his most

[2] This quotation, from *Le Pour et Contre* (IV, 39), is
here taken, like several others, from Harrisse (p. 132). Harrisse alleges extenuating circumstances for this flight (pp. 21-
22, 132-133); but his valuable biography is overindulgent and
must be used with caution. Paul Hazard's *Etudes critiques
sur Manon Lescaut* (Chicago, 1929) remains the best book
on the subject.

original work, including the *Man of Quality, Manon
Lescaut,* and much of *Cleveland.* His earnings, however, did not match his tastes. When he departed
from Holland with his mistress he left considerable
debts; and within a year he was convicted in England (December, 1733) of fabricating a bill of exchange. This would normally have sent him to the
gallows; how he got off we do not know.[3]

His banishment brought no great hardship, but his
resentment of it shows in his adopted name Prévost
d'Exiles. He was eager to regain his homeland and
religious orders. A papal brief of 1734 authorized
his transfer to a freer Benedictine congregation, and
on his return to France he was accepted (February
3, 1735) into the Abbey of La Grènetière in Vendée. His appointment as almoner to the Prince de
Conti officially dispensed him from monastic residence. He had at last a religious post that cost him
little to fill; and for the remaining twenty-eight years
of his life, with a benefice for the last nine, fill it he
did.

Though his success and his notoriety aroused envy
and reprisal (*Manon Lescaut* was banned in 1733),
Prévost's return to Paris in the autumn of 1734 was
triumphant. As one Parisian wrote, "everyone here is
fighting to get hold of him ... he would make his
fortune by just appearing at the fair." A celebrated
writer, affable, modest, witty, he was welcomed ev-
erywhere. His working pace slowed. He fell into fi-
nancial need and appealed to Frederick the Great
of Prussia, who offered hospitality but nothing more.
Early in 1741 the author of a clandestine news
sheet, whom Prévost had befriended, was arrested
and accused him of complicity. Prévost was exiled

[3] For his debts in Holland see Etienne Guilhou, *L'Abbé
Prévost en Hollande* (Groningen and Paris, 1933); for his
conviction in England, Hazard (pp. 6-7, 86), and the critical
edition of Vol. V of the *Homme de qualité,* by Mysie E. I.
Robertson (Paris, 1927).

again, but allowed to return after a year in Belgium and in Frankfurt.

His life after his return to France in 1742 was relatively uneventful. His originality had been his keen sense of youthful temptation and its dangers; the measure of his creative imagination had been given by his late thirties. He died at sixty-six on a road near Senlis, from the sudden rupture of an aneurysm, on November 25, 1763.

Some students of Prévost prefer the first edition of *Manon Lescaut* (1731), others the last (1753) that he revised and corrected.[4] Though the text used here is the latter, the case for the other is also strong. The many changes from direct statement to euphemism are, to our taste, disadvantages of the 1753 version, though appropriate to Prévost and his time. This loss is compensated, however, by increased precision and the reduction of unnecessary epithets and nouns.

Nor are the substantive changes all gains. The Des Grieux of 1753 is more contrite than that of 1731, and yet less Christian: honor and breeding now receive credit for his repentance. Manon is portrayed more compassionately: her birth is no longer modest but common—an extenuating circumstance; her infidelities are presented euphemistically; her genuine (though fair-weather) love for Des Grieux is emphasized by the new episode of the Italian prince. The shift in values from religion to honor fits the complacent, shallow moralizing of the Author's Notice. Though the 1731 version is starker, I find that of 1753 more complex and consistent.

The most interesting variants of the 1731 edition

---

[4] The majority of critics, who prefer the 1753 edition, includes Paul Hazard, editors Maurice Allem, Louis Landré, F. C. Green, M. E. I. Robertson, translators D. C. Moylan, John Manton, and L. W. Tancock. Among the champions of the 1731 text are editors Joseph Aynard and Georges Matoré and translator Helen Waddell.

appear as footnotes to the present translation, which is based on the 1753 text.

Nearly all the best work on *Manon Lescaut*—Harrisse's biography, Hazard's superlative studies, and much else—exists only in French. However, two general treatments in English can be recommended without reservation: the Introduction to Louis Landré's edition (New York, 1930) and F. C. Green's perceptive pages in *Minuet* (London, 1935).

The best English translations are those by D. C. Moylan (1841), Helen Waddell (1935), John Manton (1947), and L. W. Tancock (1949). Tancock is quite accurate; Moylan and Manton retain more of Prévost's flavor but often miss the meaning. Waddell is much the best of the four, though she uses the text (1731) that most consider not the best.

The translator's main problem here is balance. Prévost's French has a politeness, often a prettiness, that belong to his time; yet its fragrance is not archaic; it speaks directly to the modern reader. The translation must seek to reflect a man for whom, as for his time, good manners were a morality much like honesty today, and still show the quest for naturalness that Prévost expressed in this comment on his one masterpiece:

> I say nothing about the style of this work. There is neither jargon, affectation, nor sophistic reflections; it is Nature herself writing. How pitiful a starched and rouged author appears in comparison! This one does not go chasing after wit, or rather after that which is so-called. This is not a laconically constipated style but a flowing, full, and expressive one. This offers throughout nothing save portraits and feelings; but they are true portraits and natural feelings.

DONALD M. FRAME

Columbia University

A NOTE ON MONEY VALUES

20 sous=1 franc=1 livre
3 livres (francs)=1 crown
10-12 livres (francs)=1 pistole
24 livres (francs)=1 louis d'or

Story of the Chevalier des Grieux
and of
Manon Lescaut

NOTICE

by the author of the *Memoirs of a Man of Quality*

Although I might have inserted the adventures of the Chevalier des Grieux[1] into my Memoirs, it seemed to me that, there being no necessary connection, the reader would find more satisfaction in seeing them separately. An account of this length would have interrupted for too long the thread of my own story. Far as I am from claiming the quality of precision as a writer, I am not unaware that a narrative should be disencumbered of the circumstances that would make it heavy and involved. It is Horace's precept:

> What needs to be said now, let him say now,
> And put off many things for another time.[2]

Indeed there is no need of so grave an authority to prove so simple a truth; for good sense is the primary source of this rule.

If the public has found something agreeable and interesting in the story of my life, I dare promise that it will be no less satisfied with this addition. It will see, in the conduct of Monsieur des Grieux, a terrible example of the power of the passions. The man

---

[1] 1731 ed.: "the unfortunate Chevalier des Grieux."
[2] Horace, *Epistle to the Pisos (Art of Poetry)*, verses 43-44.
  Ut jam nunc dicat iam nunc debentia dici,
  Pleraque differat, ac praesens in tempus omittat.

I have to portray is one young and blind, who refuses to be happy and willfully plunges headfirst into the uttermost misfortunes; who, with all the qualities that go to make up the most brilliant merit, by his own choice prefers an obscure and vagabond life to all the advantages of fortune and nature; who foresees his miseries without wanting to avoid them; who feels them and is overwhelmed by them, without profiting by the remedies that are constantly offered him and that could end them at any moment; in short, an ambiguous character, a mixture of virtues and vices, a perpetual contrast of good sentiments and bad actions. Such is the substance of the picture I present. People of good sense will not regard a work of this nature as a useless task. Besides the pleasure of enjoyable reading, they will find in it few events that cannot serve for moral instruction; and in my opinion it is a considerable service rendered to the public to instruct while entertaining.

One cannot reflect on the principles of morality without being astonished to see them at the same time esteemed and neglected; and one wonders at the reason for this oddity of the human heart that makes it savor ideas of goodness and perfection from which it strays in practice. If people of a certain order of intelligence and breeding will examine what is the commonest substance of their conversations or even of their solitary reveries, they will easily note that these almost always turn upon certain moral considerations. The sweetest moments of their lives are those they spend, either alone or with a friend, dwelling in all candor on the charms of virtue, the delights of friendship, the ways of attaining happiness, the weaknesses of nature that keep us from it, and the remedies that can cure them. Horace and Boileau note this conversation as one of the finest features which for them make up the picture of a happy life. How then does it happen that we fall so easily from these lofty speculations and find ourselves so soon back on the level of the common run of men? I am much mistaken if the reason I am about to advance does not fully explain this contradiction between our ideas and our conduct: this is that since all moral precepts are only vague, general principles, it is very hard to apply them specifically in detail to our behavior and actions.

Let us see this thing in an example. Well-born souls feel that gentleness and humanity are attractive virtues, and are naturally inclined to practice them; but when the moment to do so comes, they often remain hesitant. Is this really the time? Do we really know how far we should go? Aren't we wrong about the recipient? A hundred difficulties stop us. We are afraid of being dupes by trying to be kind and liberal; of being considered weak by appearing too tender and emotional; in a word, of overdoing or inadequately fulfilling duties which are all too obscurely enveloped in the general notions of humanity and gentleness. In this uncertainty there is nothing but experience or example that can reasonably determine the inclinations of the heart. Now experience is not an advantage that everyone is free to gain; it depends on the different situations in which we find ourselves placed by fortune. So there remains only example that can serve for many people as a rule in the practice of virtue.

It is precisely for this sort of reader that works such as this one can be extremely useful, at least when they are written by a person of honor and good sense. Each deed that is here reported is a degree of enlightenment, an instruction that substitutes for experience; each adventure is a model on which to form oneself; all it needs is to be adjusted to the circumstances one is in. The entire work is a treatise on morality shown entertainingly in practice.

A severe reader will perhaps be offended to see me take up my pen again, at my age, to write adventures of fortune and love; but if the observation I have just made is sound, it justifies me; if it is false, my error will be my excuse.

NOTE

{on the 1753 edition}

It was to give in to the insistence of those who like this little work that we have determined to purge it of a large number of crude mistakes that have slipped into most of its editions. We have also made a few additions which seemed necessary for the plenitude of one of the principal characters.

The vignette and the pictures bear their own recommendations and praise in themselves.

STORY OF MANON LESCAUT

PART ONE

I am obliged to take my reader back to the time in my life when I first met the Chevalier des Grieux. It was about six months before I left for Spain. Although I rarely emerged from my solitude, my eagerness to please my daughter sometimes involved me in various little trips, which I kept as short as I could.

I was coming back one day from Rouen, where she had asked me to go to handle a case before the Parlement of Normandy[1] concerning the succession to certain lands to which I had left her some claims derived from my maternal grandfather. Having started back via Evreux, where I slept the first night, on the next day for dinner[2] I came to Pacy, which is about five or six leagues further. I was surprised, on entering this little town, to see all the inhabitants in an uproar. They were rushing out of their houses and running in a crowd up to the door of a wretched inn, in front of which were two covered wagons. The horses, which were still harnessed and appeared steaming with fatigue and heat, showed that these two vans had only just arrived. I stopped a moment to find out the cause of the tumult; but I derived little enlightenment from the curious crowd, which paid no attention to my inquiries and kept jostling their way toward the inn in great confusion. Finally,

[1] The twelve regional Parlements were the highest judicial bodies in France in Prévost's time.

[2] Dinner is of course the noon meal, supper the evening meal.

when an archer[3] with a bandolier and a musket on
his shoulder appeared at the door, I beckoned to
him. I asked him to tell me the cause of this uproar.

"It is nothing, sir," he told me; "it's a dozen prostitutes that my comrades and I are conducting to Le
Havre,[4] where we shall ship them to America. There
are a few pretty ones, and apparently that's what's
exciting the curiosity of these good peasants."

I would have passed on after this explanation if I
had not been stopped by the exclamations of an old
woman who was coming out of the inn wringing her
hands and crying out that it was a barbarous thing,
a thing to make you shudder and weep.

"What is it all about?" I asked her.

"Oh, sir, go in," she answered, "and see if it isn't
a sight to break your heart!"

Curiosity made me get off my horse, which I left
to my groom. I entered with difficulty, piercing the
crowd, and indeed I saw something rather touching.
Among the twelve girls who were chained by sixes
around the waist was one whose manner and face
were so incongruous with her situation that in any
other circumstances I would have taken her for a
lady of the highest rank.[5] Her sadness and the dirti-
ness of her linen and other clothes did so little to spoil
her appearance that the sight of her inspired in me
respect and pity. Nevertheless she was trying to turn
away, as far as her chain could allow, to conceal her
face from the eyes of the spectators. The effort that
she made to hide was so natural that it seemed to
come from a feeling of modesty. Since the six guards
who were escorting this unhappy band were also in
the room, I took the leader aside and asked him for
some light on the case of this beautiful girl. All he
could give me was very general.

[3] The title of these civil guards survived changes in weapons.
[4] In Prévost's text, throughout, "le Havre-de-Grâce" (the
Haven of Mercy).
[5] 1731 ed.: "for a princess."

"We took her from the Hôpital,"[6] he told me, "by order of the Lieutenant General of Police. There is nothing to suggest that she was locked up there for her good behavior. I have questioned her several times along the way: she is obstinate in refusing to answer me. But although I have received no orders to treat her any better than the others, I can't help having some consideration for her, because it seems to me she is a little better than her companions. There's a young man," added the archer, "who can inform you better than I can about the cause of her disgrace; he has followed her from Paris, crying almost every moment without stopping. He must be her brother or her lover."

I turned toward the corner of the room where this young man was sitting. He seemed buried in a deep reverie. I have never seen a more living picture of grief. He was very simply dressed; but you can tell at a glance a man of birth and education. I went over to him. He got up; and I discovered in his eyes, his face, his gestures, such a refined and noble air that I felt naturally led to wish him well.

"Do not let me disturb you," I said, sitting down beside him. "Will you please satisfy my curiosity to know about that beautiful girl, who does not seem to be made for the plight I see her in?"

He answered me civilly that he could not tell me who she was without making himself known, and that he had strong reasons for wanting to remain incognito.

"I can tell you, nevertheless, what these wretches know full well," he went on, pointing to the archers: "that I love her with a passion so violent that it makes me the most unfortunate of men. I used every

6 Known today as the Hôpital de la Salpétrière (Saltpeter-works Hospital) and used as a home for aged and mentally infirm women, in Prévost's time this institution was called the Hôpital Général and had separate parts for the needy, the insane, and prostitutes and other women judged incorrigble.
The Lieutenant General was the chief of the Paris police.

possible means in Paris to obtain her freedom. Petitions, ingenuity, force were in vain; I decided to follow her, even if I had to go to the end of the world. I will embark with her. I will go across to America. But the extreme of inhumanity is that these cowardly scoundrels," he added, speaking of the archers, "will not permit me to approach her. My plan was to attack them openly a few leagues from Paris. I had brought in four men who had promised me their help in return for a considerable sum. The traitors left me alone and at grips, and went off with my money. The impossibility of succeeding by force made me lay down my arms. I proposed to the archers that they allow me at least to follow them, offering to reward them. The desire for gain made them consent to this. They have insisted on being paid each time they granted me liberty to speak to my mistress. In a short time my purse was exhausted, and now that I am without a penny they have the barbarity to push me back brutally when I take one step toward her. Only a moment ago, when I dared approach her in spite of their threats, they had the insolence to raise the butt of their guns against me.[7] To satisfy their avarice and put myself in a position to continue on the road on foot, I am obliged to sell here a poor horse who up to now has served as my mount."

Although he seemed to tell this story rather tranquilly, he shed a few tears as he finished. This adventure seemed to me one of the most extraordinary and most touching ever.

"I do not press you," I said to him, "to disclose the secret of your affairs; but if I can be useful to you for anything, I gladly offer you my services."

"Alas!" he went on. "I do not see the faintest glimmer of hope. I must submit to the full rigor of my lot. I shall go to America. There I shall at least be free with the one I love. I have written to one of

[7] 1731 ed.: "to give me two or three hard blows with the butt of their guns."

my friends who will get some help to me at Le Havre. My only problem is how to get there, and how to procure for that poor creature," he added, looking sadly at his mistress, "some relief along the way."

"Well," I said to him, "I will solve that problem. Here is some money that I beg you to accept. I am sorry not to be able to serve you in any other way."

I gave him four louis d'or[8] without the guards' noticing it, for I clearly judged that if they knew he had that sum they would sell him their help more dear. It even occurred to me to make a bargain with them so as to obtain for the young lover the freedom to talk to his mistress continually all the way to Le Havre. I signaled to the leader to approach, and I proposed this to him. He seemed ashamed of it, in spite of his effrontery.

"It is not, sir," he replied in an embarrassed manner, "that we refuse to let him speak to this girl; but he would like to be with her all the time; that is inconvenient for us; it is quite fair that he should pay for the inconvenience."

"Let's just see," I said to him, "what would be needed to keep you from feeling it."

He had the audacity to ask me for two louis. I gave them to him on the spot.

"But take care," I said to him, "that you don't allow yourself any trickery, for I shall leave this young man my address so that he can inform me of any, and be assured that I shall have the power to have you punished."

The whole thing cost me six louis d'or. The graciousness and the heartfelt gratitude with which this young unknown thanked me confirmed my conviction that he was born somebody and that he deserved my liberality. I said a few words to his mistress before

---

[8] A gold coin worth 24 livres, bearing the effigy of the king of France. For the relative worth of all money mentioned throughout this book, see "A Note on Money Values," p. XV.

going out. She answered me with such sweet and charming modesty that as I left I could not help making a thousand reflections on the incomprehensible character of women.

Having gone back to my solitude, I was not informed of the sequel to this adventure. Nearly two years passed, which made me forget it completely, until chance revived the opportunity for me to learn all the circumstances in full detail.

I was arriving in Calais from London with the marquis of . . . , my pupil. We stayed, if I remember rightly, at the Golden Lion, where for certain reasons we were obliged to spend the entire day and the following night. Walking through the streets in the afternoon, I thought I noticed that same young man whom I had met at Pacy. He was very poorly dressed and much paler than I had seen him to be the first time. He was carrying an old portmanteau by hand, having just arrived in town. However, since he had too handsome a face not to be easily recognized, I immediately remembered him.

"We must speak to that young man," I said to the marquis.

His joy was keen beyond expression when he recognized me in turn.

"Ah! sir," he cried, kissing my hand, "so I can express to you once again my undying gratitude!"

I asked him where he was coming from. He answered that he had just arrived by sea from Le Havre, where he had landed from America a little before.

"You don't seem very well off for money," I said to him. "Go along to the Golden Lion, where I am staying. I'll join you in a moment."

I went back there indeed full of impatience to learn the details of his misfortune and the circumstances of his trip to America. I showed him every sign of affection and gave orders that he should lack nothing. He did not wait for me to urge him to tell me the story of his life.

"Sir," he said to me, "you treat me so nobly that I would reproach myself with base ingratitude if I kept anything secret from you. I want to let you know not only my misfortunes and sufferings, but also my excesses and my most shameful weaknesses. I am sure that while you condemn me you will not be able to help pitying me."

Here I must notify the reader that I wrote down his story almost as soon as I heard it, and that one may consequently be assured that nothing could be more accurate and faithful than this narrative—I say faithful, even in reporting the reflections and feelings which this young adventurer expressed with the best grace in the world. So here is his story, to which, from beginning to end, I shall add nothing that is not his own.

I was seventeen and I was finishing my philosophy course at Amiens, where my parents, who belong to one of the best families in P . . . , had sent me. I was leading such a docile and orderly life that my masters held me up as a model to the school. It was not that I made any extraordinary efforts to deserve this praise, but my temperament is naturally gentle and tranquil; I applied myself to study by inclination, and certain signs of a natural aversion toward vice were accounted to me as virtues. My birth, my success in my studies, and certain attractive external qualities[9] had made me known and esteemed by all the good people in the town. I completed my public examinations with such general approbation that the bishop, who was present, suggested that I make my career in the Church, where I would not fail, he said, to acquire more distinction than in the Order of Malta, for which my parents destined me. They had me already wearing the cross, with the title Chevalier des Grieux.

When vacation came, I was preparing to go home

9 1731 ed.: "certain good natural qualities."

to my father's, who had promised to send me soon to the Academy.[10] My only regret in leaving Amiens was leaving behind a friend to whom I had always been tenderly attached. He was a few years older than I. We had been brought up together, but since his family had only the most modest means he was obliged to enter the Church and stay on at Amiens after me to do the studying appropriate to that profession. He had a thousand good qualities. You will come to know him by the best of these later on in my story, and especially by a zeal and generosity in friendship that surpass the most famous examples from antiquity. If I had followed his advice then, I would have been always wise and happy. If I had at least profited by his reproaches in the abyss into which my passions dragged me, I would have saved something from the wreck of my fortune and my reputation. But he gained no other fruit from his cares than the pain of seeing them useless and sometimes harshly repaid by an ingrate who took offense at them and treated them as importunities.

I had set the date for leaving Amiens. Alas! Why did I not set it one day earlier! I would have returned to my father's house with all my innocence. The very day before I was to leave that town, as I was taking a walk with my friend, whose name was Tiberge, we saw the Arras coach arrive, and we followed it to the inn where these carriages stop. We had no other motive than curiosity. A few women got out, and immediately went off. But one remained, very young, who stayed alone in the courtyard while an elderly man, who seemed to be acting as her escort, was doing his best to have her baggage taken out of the racks. She seemed to me so charming that I, who had never thought about the difference between the sexes or looked at a girl with any attention, I (I say), at whose good conduct and restraint everyone wondered, found myself all at once trans-

[10] An academy in Paris training young gentlemen in horsemanship, dancing, music, and fencing.

ported and on fire. I had the defect of being excessively timid and easily disconcerted; but far from being stopped then by this weakness, I advanced toward the mistress of my heart.

Although she was even younger than I, she received my civilities without seeming embarrassed. I asked her what brought her to Amiens and whether there were people she knew there. She answered straightforwardly that she was sent there by her parents to become a nun. Love had already so enlightened me, in the moment it had been in my heart, that I regarded this plan as a mortal blow to my desires. I spoke to her in a way that made her understand my feelings; for she was far more experienced than I. It was in spite of her that she was being sent to a convent, no doubt to check her inclination to pleasure, which had already manifested itself and which later caused all her misfortunes and mine. I opposed her parents' cruel intention with all the reasons that my newborn love and my scholastic eloquence could suggest. She made no pretense of either rigor or disdain; she told me after a moment of silence that she foresaw only too well that she was going to be unhappy; but that it was apparently the will of Heaven, since Heaven left her no way to avoid it. The sweetness of her glances, a charming air of sadness as she uttered these words, or rather the power of my destiny, which was dragging me on to my ruin, did not let me hesitate a moment over my answer. I assured her that if she would place some reliance on my honor and on the infinite tenderness that she already inspired in me, I would devote my life to delivering her from the tyranny of her parents and to making her happy. A thousand times since I have been astonished, on thinking where I then got so much boldness and facility in expression; but men would not make a divinity of Love if it did not often work miracles.

I added a thousand urgent things. My lovely unknown well knew that a man is not a deceiver at

my age; she confessed to me that if I could see any
way of setting her free she would think herself be-
holden to me for something dearer than life itself. I
repeated to her that I was ready to undertake anything, but, not having enough experience to imagine
instantly a way to serve her, I confined myself to
this general assurance, which could be of no great
help to her or to me.

Her old Argus[11] having come back and joined us,
my hopes would have miscarried if she had not had
enough wit to make up for the sterility of mine. I was
surprised, on the arrival of her escort, that she called
me her cousin and that, without seeming the least
bit disconcerted, she told me that since she was so
fortunate as to run across me in Amiens, she was
putting off going into the convent until the next day
so as to give herself the pleasure of having supper
with me. I readily entered into the spirit of this ruse;
I suggested that she stay at an inn where the master,
who had set up in business in Amiens after long
being my father's coachman, was entirely devoted to
my orders. I took her there myself, while the old
escort seemed to murmur a bit and while my friend
Tiberge, who understood nothing of this scene, followed me without uttering a word. He had not heard
our conversation. He had remained walking about
the courtyard while I was talking of love to my
beautiful mistress. Since I feared his wisdom, I got
rid of him by an errand I asked him to do. Thus I
had the pleasure, on arriving at the inn, of talking
alone with the sovereign of my heart.

I soon recognized that I was less of a child than I
supposed. My heart opened to a thousand pleasurable
feelings of which I had never had an idea. A sweet
warmth spread through all my veins. I was in a kind
of ecstasy which for a time took away my ability to
speak and expressed itself only by my eyes. Mademoiselle Manon Lescaut (this she told me was her

11 A legendary character with a thousand eyes.

name) seemed very satisfied with this effect of her charms. I thought I noticed that she was no less affected than I. She confessed to me that she found me attractive and that she would be enchanted to owe her freedom to me. She wanted to know who I was, and this knowledge increased her affection; for, being of common birth,[12] she felt flattered at her conquest of a lover such as I.

We discussed means of belonging to each other. After many reflections, we found no other way than flight. We had to elude the vigilance of her escort, who was a man to be reckoned with, although he was only a servant. We decided that during the night I would have a post chaise made ready and would return to the inn very early in the morning before he was awake; that we would steal away secretly and go straight to Paris, where we would be married on arrival. I had about fifty crowns, which were the fruit of my little savings; she had about twice that. We imagined, like inexperienced children, that this sum would never be used up, and we counted no less on the success of our other measures.

After having supper with more satisfaction than I had ever felt, I withdrew to carry out our plan. My arrangements were all the easier because, having intended to return to my father's the next day, I had my few things already packed. So I had no trouble in having my trunk picked up and a chaise held ready for five o'clock in the morning, which was the time when the town gates were to be opened; but I found one obstacle I had not anticipated, which nearly broke up my plan completely.

Tiberge, although only three years older than I, was a youth of mature sense and very orderly conduct. He loved me with extraordinary tenderness. The sight of a girl as pretty as Mademoiselle Manon, my eagerness to escort her, and the care I had taken to get rid of him by sending him off, roused in him

---

[12] 1731 ed.: "for, not being of rank although of rather good birth."

some suspicion of my love. He had not dared to come back to the inn, where he had left me, for fear of offending me by returning; but he had gone to wait for me at my lodgings, where I found him when I arrived, although it was ten o'clock in the evening. His presence vexed me. He easily perceived the constraint that it caused me.

"I am sure," he said to me without concealment, "that you are meditating some plan that you want to hide from me; I see it by your manner."

I answered him rather brusquely that I was not obliged to give him an account of all my plans.

"No," he went on, "but you have always treated me as a friend, and that quality implies some little confidence and openness."

He pressed me so hard and so long to reveal my secret that, having never had any reserve with him, I made a clean breast of my passion to him. He heard me with a look of disapproval that made me tremble. I especially repented the indiscretion with which I had disclosed to him my plan for flight. He told me that he was too completely my friend not to oppose it with all his power; that he wanted first to make me see everything that he thought might possibly change my mind; but that if I then did not give up this miserable resolution he would inform people who could surely put a stop to it. He gave me a serious talk about that, which lasted more than a quarter of an hour and which also concluded with the threat of denouncing me if I did not give him my word to behave more sensibly and rationally. I was in despair at having betrayed myself so inopportunely. However, since love had opened my mind wide in the last two or three hours, I realized that I had not revealed to him that my plan was to be carried out the next day, and I resolved to deceive him with the help of equivocation.

"Tiberge," I said to him, "I believed until now that you were my friend, and I wanted to test you by this confidence. It is true that I am in love, I have not deceived you; but as regards my flight, that is not a thing to undertake at random. Come and pick me up tomorrow at nine o'clock; I will show you my mistress, if this can be done, and you shall judge whether she deserves my taking this step for her."

He left me alone after a thousand protestations of friendship. I spent the night putting my affairs in order, and, having gone around dawn to Mademoiselle Manon's inn, I found her waiting for me. She was at her window, which opened on the street, so that when she saw me she came and opened the door for me herself. We went out without a sound. She had no other baggage than her linen, which I carried myself. The chaise was ready to leave; we immediately sped away from the town.

Later on I will relate how Tiberge behaved when he found that I had deceived him. His zeal became no less ardent. You will see to what extremes he carried it and how many tears I should shed when I think what its reward has always been.

We had made such haste to get on that we reached Saint-Denis before nightfall. I had raced along on horseback beside the chaise, which had scarcely allowed us to exchange a word except when we changed horses; but when we saw ourselves so near Paris, that is to say almost in safety, we took the time to refresh ourselves, having eaten nothing since we left Amiens. Passionate as I was for Manon, she succeeded in persuading me that she was no less so for me. We were so unreserved in our caresses that we did not have the patience to wait until we were alone. Our postilions and hosts looked at us with wonder; and I noticed that they were surprised to see two children of our age who seemed madly in love with each other. Our plans for marriage were forgotten at Saint-Denis; we defrauded the Church of its rights; and we found ourselves man and wife without giving the matter a thought.

It is certain that with my tender and constant nature I would have been happy for life, if Manon had been faithful to me. The more I knew her, the more new qualities I found in her to love. Her wit, her heart, her sweetness, and her beauty formed so strong and so charming a chain that I would have set my whole happiness in never escaping from it. What a terrible change! What causes my despair could have caused my bliss. I find myself the most unhappy of all men through that very constancy from which I had reason to expect the sweetest of all destinies and the most perfect rewards of love.

We took a furnished apartment in Paris. It was on the Rue V . . .[13] and, for my misfortune, next to the house of Monsieur de B . . . , a famous farmer-general. Three weeks passed, during which I had been so full of my passion that I had thought but little of my family and of the chagrin that my father must have felt at my absence. However, since debauch had no part in my conduct and since Manon too was behaving with much restraint, the tranquillity in which we lived served to remind me little by little of my sense of duty. I resolved to be reconciled, if possible, with my father. My mistress was so attractive that I had no doubt she could win him over if I could find a way to make him know her good sense and merit: in a word, I flattered myself that I could get his permission to marry her, having been disabused of my hope of doing so without his consent.

I communicated this plan to Manon and made her understand that besides the motives of love and duty, that of necessity might count for something too, for our funds were extremely depleted and I was beginning to revise my opinion that they were inexhaustible.

Manon received this proposition coldly. However, since the difficulties that she raised were derived only from her very tenderness and the fear of losing me —in case my father, after learning the location of our retreat, did not enter into our plan—I had not

[13] Probably the Rue Vivienne, near the old stock exchange, in what was then the most fashionable part of Paris.

the slightest suspicion of the cruel blow that was being prepared for me. To the objection of necessity,
she answered that we still had enough to live on for
a few weeks and that after that she would find resources in the affection of certain out-of-town relatives to whom she would write. She softened her
refusal by caresses so tender and passionate that I,
who lived in her alone and who had not the slightest
mistrust of her heart, applauded all her answers and
all her resolutions.

I had left to her the disposal of our money and
the task of paying our ordinary expenses. I perceived
a little later that our table was better furnished and
that she had treated herself to some quite expensive
finery. Since I was not unaware that we must have
barely twelve or fifteen pistoles left, I showed my
astonishment at this apparent increase in our opulence. She begged me, laughing, not to worry about
it.

"Didn't I promise you," she said to me, "that I'd
find resources?"

I loved her with too much simplicity to take alarm
easily.

One day when I had gone out in the afternoon
and had told her I would be out longer than usual,
I was astonished on my return to be kept waiting
two or three minutes at the door. Our only servant
was a girl of about our own age. When she came
and let me in I asked her why she had been so long.
She answered in an embarrassed way that she had
not heard me knock. I had knocked only once; I
said to her:

"But if you didn't hear me, then why did you
come to let me in?"

This question so disconcerted her that, not having
enough presence of mind to answer it, she began to
cry, assuring me that it was not her fault and that
Madame had forbidden her to open the door until
Monsieur de B . . . had left by the other stairs, which
connected with the boudoir. I remained so taken

aback that I had not the strength to enter the apartment. I made up my mind to go back downstairs on the pretext of an errand, and I ordered the child to tell her mistress that I would be back in a moment, but not to let her know that she had told me about Monsieur de B. . . .

My consternation was so great that I was shedding tears as I went down the stairs, without knowing yet what feeling prompted them. I went into the nearest coffeehouse and, sitting down at a table, I buried my head in both my hands to unravel what was going on in my heart. I did not dare recall what I had just heard. I wanted to consider it as an illusion; and two or three times I was ready to go back to the house without indicating that I had paid any attention to it. It seemed to me so impossible that Manon had betrayed me that I was afraid of insulting her by suspecting her. I adored her, that was certain; I had given her no more proofs of love than I had received from her; why should I have accused her of being less sincere and less constant than I? What reason would she have had to deceive me? Only three hours before, she had loaded me with her tenderest caresses and received mine with the same transports; I knew my own heart no better than I did hers.

"No, no," I continued, "it is not possible that Manon is betraying me. She is not unaware that I live only for her. She knows too well that I adore her. That is no reason for her to hate me."

However, the visit and the furtive departure of Monsieur de B . . . caused me some anxiety. I also remembered Manon's little acquisitions, which seemed to me to go beyond our present riches. That seemed to smack of the liberalities of a new lover. And that confidence that she had shown me in resources that were unknown to me! I had difficulty in assigning to so many enigmas as favorable a meaning as my heart desired. On the other hand, she had scarcely been out of my sight since we had been in Paris. Occupations, walks, diver-

sions—we had always been at each other's side. Good
Lord! A moment of separation would have distressed us
too much. We had to be telling each other unceasingly
that we loved each other; we would have died of
anxiety without that. So I could scarcely imagine a
single moment when Manon could have occupied herself with any other man. Finally I thought I had
found the solution to this mystery.

"Monsieur de B . . . ," I said to myself, "is a man
who handles big affairs and has great connections;
Manon's relatives must have used this man to get
some money to her. She may have received some
from him already; he came today to bring her more.
No doubt she has made a game of hiding it from
me so as to give me a pleasant surprise. Perhaps
she would have spoken to me about it if I had come
in as usual instead of coming here and making myself miserable. At least she will not hide this from
me when I speak to her about it myself."

I filled myself so stoutly with this opinion that it
had the power to diminish my sadness greatly. I
went back to the house immediately. I kissed Manon
with my usual tenderness. She received me very well.
I was tempted at first to reveal to her my conjectures,
which more than ever I regarded as certain; I restrained
myself, in the hope that she might make the first move
and tell me everything that had happened.

Supper was served to us. I sat down to table with
a very gay air; but by the light of the candle that
was between her and me I thought I detected sadness on the face and in the eyes of my dear mistress. This thought inspired in me some sadness too.
I noted that her glances clung to me in a different
way than they usually had. I could not make out
whether it was love or compassion, although it
seemed to me that it was a sweet and languorous
feeling. I looked at her with the same attention; and
perhaps she had no less difficulty in judging, from
my glances, the situation of my heart. We had no

thought of either speaking or eating. Finally I saw
tears fall from her beautiful eyes: perfidious tears!

"Oh Gods!" I exclaimed. "You are weeping, my
dear Manon; you are distressed enough to weep, and
you tell me not a single word of your troubles."

She answered me only by a few sighs which increased my anxiety. I rose, trembling. I conjured her,
with all the solicitude of love, to reveal to me the
reason for her tears; I shed some myself while dry-
ing hers; I was more dead than alive. A barbarian
would have been touched by the tokens of my grief
and fear.

During the time that I was thus occupied entirely
with her, I heard the sound of several people coming up
the stairs. There was a soft knock on the door. Manon
gave me a kiss and, slipping out of my arms, went
swiftly into the boudoir and closed the door behind
her. I imagined that, being a little disarrayed, she
wanted to hide from the eyes of the strangers who
had knocked. I went and opened the door for them
myself. Hardly had I opened it when I found myself seized by three men whom I recognized as lackeys of my father. They did me no violence; but,
two of them having seized me by the arms, the third
searched my pockets and took out a little knife that
was the only weapon I had on me. They asked my
pardon for the necessity they were under of treating
me with this lack of respect; they told me, most
naturally, that they were acting on my father's orders, and that my elder brother was waiting for me
in a carriage below. I was so upset that I let myself
be led away without resistance or reply. My brother was indeed waiting for me. I was put into the
carriage next to him, and the coachman, who had
his orders, drove us at top speed to Saint-Denis. My
brother embraced me tenderly, but did not speak to
me, so that I had all the leisure I needed for meditating about my misfortune.

I found so much obscurity in it at first that I saw
no light in the slightest conjecture. I was cruelly be-

trayed. But by whom? Tiberge was the first who came to my mind. "Traitor," I said to myself, "your life is finished if my suspicions are founded." However, I reflected that he did not know where I lived, and that consequently this could not have been learned from him. As for accusing Manon, my heart dared not make itself guilty of that. The extraordinary sadness with which I had seen her virtually overwhelmed, her tears, the tender kiss she had given me as she withdrew, did indeed seem an enigma to me; but I felt inclined to explain it as a presentiment of our common disaster, and, in the very time that I was despairing over the accident that tore me away from her, I had the credulity to imagine that she was even more to be pitied than I.

The result of my meditation was to persuade me that I had been seen in the streets of Paris by certain acquaintances who had notified my father. This thought consoled me. I was counting on getting off with reproaches or some harsh treatment which I would have to take from my father's authority. I resolved to suffer them patiently and to promise whatever should be required of me, in order to facilitate my chances of going back to Paris more promptly and restoring life and joy to my dear Manon.

In a short time we arrived at Saint-Denis. My brother, surprised at my silence, imagined that it was an effect of fear. He undertook to console me, assuring me that I had nothing to dread from my father's severity, provided I was disposed to return quietly to the path of duty and to merit the affection he had for me. He had me spend the night at Saint-Denis, with the precaution of having the three lackeys sleep in my room. What gave me great pain was to find myself in the same inn where I had stopped with Manon on our way from Amiens to Paris. The host and the servants recognized me and in the same moment guessed the truth about my story. I heard the host say:

"Oh! That's that nice-looking gentleman who was

passing through six weeks ago with a little lady he was so much in love with. How charming she was! Poor children, how they caressed each other! My word, it's a pity they've been separated."

I pretended to hear nothing, and showed myself as little as I could.

At Saint-Denis my brother had a chaise for two, in which we left early in the morning and reached home the next day in the evening. He saw my father before I did, to try to win him over by telling him how gently I had let myself be brought home; so that I was less harshly received by him than I had expected. He contented himself with some general reproaches on the offense I had committed by absenting myself without his permission. As regarded my mistress, he told me I had richly deserved what had just happened to me by giving myself up to an unknown woman; that he had had a better opinion of my prudence, but that he hoped this little adventure would make me wiser. I took this talk only in the sense that fitted in with my own ideas. I thanked my father for his kindness in forgiving me, and I promised to adopt a more submissive and more disciplined behavior. In the bottom of my heart I was triumphant, for from the way things were shaping up I had no doubt that I should be free to escape from the house even before the night was over.

We sat down to supper. I was twitted about my Amiens conquest and my flight with this faithful mistress. I took my beating with good grace. I was even delighted to be allowed to talk about what continually occupied my mind. But a few words that my father let slip made me lend my ear with the utmost attention. He spoke of perfidy and of a self-serving favor done him by Monsieur B . . .[14] I remained nonplussed on hearing him utter that name, and I humbly begged him to explain himself further. He turned to my brother and asked him if he had not told me the

[14] From this point on Prévost refers to Monsieur de B. . . as Monsieur B. . . .

whole story. My brother answered that I had seemed so quiet on the road that he had not thought I needed that remedy to cure me of my folly. I noted that my father was hesitating whether to complete his explanation. I begged him so insistently to do so that he satisfied me, or rather cruelly murdered me, with the most horrible story ever told.

He asked me first whether I had always been simple enough to believe I was loved by my mistress. I told him boldly that I was so sure of it that nothing could make me lose the least bit of my trust.

"Ha, ha, ha!" he exclaimed, laughing with all his might. "That's excellent! You're a fine dupe, and I like to see those sentiments in you. It's a great pity, my poor Chevalier, to put you into the Order of Malta, since you have so much aptitude for making a patient and accommodating husband."

He added a thousand mockeries of the same caliber about what he called my stupidity and my credulity. Finally, as I remained silent, he went on to tell me that, according to the best calculation he could make about the time since I left Amiens, Manon had loved me for about twelve days.

"For," he added, "I know that you left Amiens on the 28th of last month; it is now the 29th of this month; it was eleven days ago that Monsieur B . . . wrote me; I suppose he needed eight to come to a perfect understanding[15] with your mistress; so if you take eleven and eight from the thirty-one days between the 28th of one month and the 29th of the next, it leaves twelve, give or take a little."

Thereupon the gales of laughter began again. I listened to it all with a sense of something clutching at my heart which I feared I could not resist until the end of this sad comedy.

"You shall know then," my father went on, "since you do not, that Monsieur B . . . has won the heart

[15] 1731 ed.: "to form a perfect friendship."

of your princess; for he is trying to make a fool of me when he aims to convince me that it was out of disinterested zeal to serve me that he wanted to take her away from you. He is certainly just the sort of man—who incidentally does not know me—from whom to expect such noble sentiments! He learned from her that you are my son; and to rid himself of your importunities he wrote me where you lived and the disorderly life you were living, giving me to understand that force would be needed to make sure of you. He offered to facilitate ways of getting you by the neck, and it was by his directions and those of your mistress herself that your brother found a moment to catch you unawares. Now congratulate yourself on the duration of your triumph. You know how to conquer pretty rapidly, Chevalier, but you don't know how to preserve your conquests."[16]

I had not the strength to endure any longer a talk every word of which pierced my heart. I rose from the table, and I had not taken four steps to leave the room when I fell on the floor senseless and unconscious. Prompt aid restored me to my senses. I opened my eyes only to shed a torrent of tears, and my mouth only to utter the saddest and most touching laments. My father, who has always loved me tenderly, used all his affection to console me. I listened to him, but without hearing him. I threw myself at his knees; I conjured him, clasping my hands, to let me return to Paris and go and put a dagger into B. . . .

"No," I said, "he has not won Manon's heart, he has done her violence; he has seduced her by some charm or poison; he may have brutally forced her. Manon loves me. Don't I know that well? He must have threatened her, dagger in hand, in order to constrain her to abandon me. What must he not have done to rob me of so charming a mistress! Ye

[16] This is Maharbal's famous remark to Hannibal (as reported by Livy, Book XXII, ch. 5) after Hannibal's defeat of the Romans at Cannae.

Gods! Ye Gods! Could it be possible for Manon to have betrayed me and stopped loving me!"

Since I kept talking about going right back to Paris, and getting up every moment to do so, my father saw clearly that in the transports I was in nothing would be capable of stopping me. He took me to an upper room, where he left two servants with me to keep an eye on me. I was beside myself. I would have given a thousand lives to be in Paris for a quarter of an hour. I understood that since I had declared myself so openly, I would not easily be allowed to leave my room. I measured the height of the windows with my eyes; seeing no possibility of escaping by that route, I addressed my two servants gently. I promised, with a thousand vows, to make their fortune some day if they would consent to my getting away. I urged them, I cajoled them, I threatened them; but this attempt was also useless. Then I lost all hope. I resolved to die, and I threw myself on a bed, intending never to leave it alive.

I spent the night and the following day in this situation. I refused the food that was brought me the next morning. In the afternoon my father came to see me. He was kind enough to soothe my grief by the gentlest consolations. He ordered me so flatly to eat something that I did so out of respect for his orders. A few days passed, during which I ate nothing except in his presence and out of obedience to him. He still kept bringing up arguments aimed at restoring me to my senses and filling me with contempt for the faithless Manon. It is certain that I no longer esteemed her: how could I have esteemed the most fickle and perfidious of all creatures? But the picture of her, the charming features that I bore in my inmost heart, still remained. I was quite aware of it.

"I may die," I said; "I even should, after so much shame and pain; but I would suffer a thousand deaths without being able to forget the ungrateful Manon."

My father was surprised to see that I was still so

strongly affected. He knew I had honorable principles; and, unable to doubt that her treachery must
make me despise her, he fancied that my constancy
came less from this passion in particular than from
a general attraction to women. He attached himself
so to this idea that, consulting only his tender affection, he came one day and broached the idea to
me.

"Chevalier," he said to me, "I have planned up
to now to have you wear the Cross of Malta; but I
see that your inclinations do not point at all in that
direction. You are fond of pretty women. My notion
is to find you one you like. Tell me candidly what
you think of that."

I answered that I no longer made any distinction
between women, and that after the misfortune I had
just experienced I detested them all alike.

"I'll find you one," my father went on, smiling,
"who will look like Manon and be more faithful."

"Ah! If you feel kindly disposed toward me," I
said to him, "she is the one you must give me back.
Rest assured, my dear father, she has not betrayed
me; she is incapable of such black and cruel baseness. It is the perfidious B . . . who is deceiving us
all: you, her, and me. If you knew how tender and
sincere she is, if you knew her, you would love her
yourself."

"You are a child," my father retorted. "How can
you blind yourself to such a point after what I have
told you about her? It was she herself who delivered
you up to your brother. You should forget even her
name, and take advantage, if you are wise, of my
indulgence toward you."

I recognized only too clearly that he was right. It
was an involuntary impulse that made me thus side
with my faithless love.

"Alas!" I said after a moment of silence. "It is
only too true that I am the unhappy object of the
basest of all perfidies. Yes," I went on, shedding
tears of vexation, "I see very well that I am only a

child. It cost them little to deceive my credulity. But I know very well what I have to do to take revenge."

My father wanted to know what my plan was.

"I shall go to Paris," I told him, "I shall set fire to B . . . 's house, and I shall burn him alive with the perfidious Manon."

This outburst made my father laugh and served only to have me guarded more closely in my prison.

I spent six whole months there, during the first of which there was little change in my state of mind. All my feelings were just a perpetual alternation between hatred and love, hope and despair, according to the idea of Manon that came to my mind. Now I considered in her only the most lovable of all girls and I languished with desire to see her again; now I saw in her only a base and perfidious mistress and I made a thousand vows to seek her out only in order to punish her.

I was given books, which served to restore a little tranquillity to my soul. I reread all my authors; I acquired new knowledge; I regained[17] an infinite fondness for study. You will see what use it was to me later on. The enlightenment I owed to love cleared up for me a quantity of passages in Horace and Virgil that had seemed obscure to me before. I wrote a lover's commentary on the fourth book of the *Aeneid;* I plan to publish it, and I flatter myself that the public will be satisfied with it.

"Alas!" I would say as I worked on it. "What the faithful Dido needed was a heart like mine."

Tiberge came to see me one day in my prison. I was surprised at the transport with which he embraced me. I had as yet had no proofs of his affection that could make me regard it as anything but an ordinary school friendship such as springs up between young fellows of about the same age. I found him so changed and so matured, in the five or six months I

[17] 1731 ed.: "I gained."

had spent without seeing him, that his face and the tone of his talk filled me with respect. He spoke to me as a wise counselor rather than as a school friend. He lamented my fall and my straying from the right path. He congratulated me on my cure, which he thought well advanced; finally he exhorted me to profit by this youthful error and open my eyes to the vanity of pleasures. I looked at him with astonishment. He noticed it.

"My dear Chevalier," he said to me, "I am telling you nothing that is not solid truth and of which I have not convinced myself by serious examination. I had as much inclination toward sensual pleasure as you; but Heaven had given me at the same time a taste for virtue. I used my reason to compare the fruits of each of these, and it did not take me long to discover their differences. The help of Heaven supported my reflections. I have formed a contempt for the world that nothing can equal.

"Can you guess what keeps me in it," he added, "and prevents me from hastening into solitude? It is solely my warm friendship for you. I know the excellence of your heart and mind; there is nothing good of which you cannot make yourself capable. The poison of pleasure has made you leave the right road. What a loss for virtue! Your flight from Amiens caused me so much sorrow that I have not enjoyed a single moment of satisfaction since. Judge for yourself by the steps it made me take."

He told me that after recognizing that I had deceived him and left with my mistress, he had taken horse to follow me; but since I had four or five hours' headstart on him, it had been impossible for him to catch up to me; nevertheless he had reached Saint-Denis a half hour after I had left; being quite sure that I would stay in Paris, he had spent six weeks there looking for me in vain; he had gone to all the places where he was confident he could find me, and at last one day he had recognized my mistress at the Comédie Française; she was so dazzlingly

arrayed that he had had the notion that she owed
this wealth to a new lover; he had followed her carriage to her house and learned from a servant that
she was liberally kept by Monsieur B. . . .

"I did not stop there," he went on. "I went back
there the next day to learn from her own lips what
had become of you: she left me abruptly when she
heard me speak of you, and I was obliged to come
back to the country with no further light on the matter. There I learned of your adventure and the extreme consternation it has caused you; but I did not
want to see you until I could be assured of finding
you calmer."

"So you've seen Manon," I answered him with a
sigh. "Alas! You are more fortunate than I, who am
condemned never to see her again."

He reproached me for that sigh, which still showed
my weakness for her. He flattered me so adroitly on
the goodness of my character and on my inclinations
that he aroused in me, from this first visit, a strong
desire to renounce, like him, all the pleasures of the
world and enter holy orders.

I enjoyed this idea so much that when I was alone
I thought of nothing else. I remembered the words
of the bishop of Amiens, who had given me the same
advice, and the happy prospects he had envisioned
for me if I decided to embrace this plan. Piety also
joined in my considerations.

"I will lead a good Christian life,"[18] I would say
to myself; "I will occupy myself with study and religion, which will not allow me to think of the dangerous pleasures of love. I will scorn what the generality
of men admire, and, since I feel sure enough that my
heart will desire only what it esteems, I shall have as
few worries as desires."

On this as a base I planned in advance a peaceful and solitary system of life. I brought into it a

18 1731 ed.: "a simple Christian life." The 1753 edition reads,
in the text, "a holy and Christian life"; but the Errata corrects
"holy" to read "good" or "wise" (*sage*).

sequestered house, with a little wood, and a stream of fresh water at the end of the garden; a library composed of choice books, a small number of virtuous and sensible friends, a neat but frugal and moderate table. To this I added a correspondence with a friend who would be living in Paris and who would keep me informed about public affairs, less to satisfy my curiosity than to afford me the diverting spectacle of the mad agitations of men. "Shall I not be happy?" I would add. "Will not all my aspirations be fulfilled?" It is certain that this plan was most flattering to my inclinations. But after constructing so wise an arrangement, I could feel that my heart was still waiting for something else, and that in order to leave nothing to be desired in the most charming of solitudes, I had to be there with Manon.

However, as Tiberge continued to pay me frequent visits, with the aim that he had now inspired in me, I took the occasion to broach the matter to my father. He declared that it was his intention to leave his children free to choose their career and that, whatever plan I might wish to make for myself, he would reserve for himself only the right to help me by his advice. This he gave me, and very wise, which tended less to spoil my taste for my plan than to make me embrace it with more knowledge. The beginning of the academic year was approaching. I agreed with Tiberge that we would both enter the Seminary of Saint-Sulpice,[19] he to complete his theological studies, and I to begin mine. His merit, which was known to the bishop of the diocese, caused him to obtain a considerable benefice from that prelate before we left.

My father, thinking me quite recovered from my passion, made no difficulty over letting me go. We arrived in Paris. The ecclesiastical gown replaced the Cross of Malta, and the name Abbé des Grieux that of Chevalier. I devoted myself to study with so much

---

[19] A famous institution for training priests, near the square and the church of Saint-Sulpice in Paris.

application that I made extraordinary progress within a few months. I spent part of the night at it, and I did not lose a moment of the day. My reputation was so dazzling that people were already congratulating me on the dignities that I could not fail to obtain; and without my soliciting it, my name was inscribed on the benefice list. Nor was piety any more neglected; I had a fervor for all the devotional exercises. Tiberge was delighted with what he regarded as his handiwork, and many times I have seen him shed tears in delight at what he called my conversion.

That human resolutions are subject to change is a fact that has never caused me any astonishment; one passion engenders them, another passion can destroy them; but when I think of the holiness of those that had led me to Saint-Sulpice and the inward joy that Heaven granted me as I carried them out, I am terrified at the ease with which I could break them. If it is true that heavenly aid is at every moment equal in strength to the passions, then let someone explain to me by what fatal influence we can find ourselves swept all of a sudden far away from our duty without finding ourselves capable of the slightest resistance and without feeling the slightest remorse. I thought I was absolutely delivered from the weaknesses of love. It seemed to me that I would have preferred reading a page of Saint Augustine or a quarter of an hour of Christian meditation to all the pleasures of the senses, not excepting those that would have been offered me by Manon. However, one unhappy moment plunged me back over the precipice; and my fall was all the more irreparable because, finding myself all of a sudden at the same depth from which I had issued before, the new disorders into which I fell carried me down much further still toward the bottom of the abyss.

I had spent almost a year in Paris without inquiring about Manon's affairs. At first it had cost me much effort to do myself this violence; but the ever-present counsels of Tiberge and my own reflections had won me the victory. The last months had flowed past so tranquilly that I thought I was on the point of eternally forgetting that charming and perfidious creature. The time came when I was to undergo a public examination[20] in the School of Theology. I invited several distinguished people to honor me with their presence. Thus my name was spread into every quarter of Paris: it even reached the ears of my faithless Manon. She did not recognize it for certain under the title of Abbé; but a remnant of curiosity, or perhaps some repentance for having betrayed me (I have never been able to make out which of these two feelings), made her take an interest in a name so similar to mine; she came to the Sorbonne with a few other ladies. She was present at my disputation, and no doubt she had little trouble in placing me.

I had not the slightest knowledge of this visit. You know that in these places there are private alcoves for ladies, where they are hidden behind a screen. I went back to Saint-Sulpice covered with glory and loaded with compliments.

It was six in the evening. A moment after I got back I was notified that a lady was asking to see me. I went to the parlor right away. Ye Gods! What an astounding apparition! There I found Manon. It was she, but lovelier and more dazzling than I had ever seen her. She was in her eighteenth year. Her charms surpassed all possible description. Her manner was so elegant, so sweet, so attractive! the manner of Love itself. Her whole face seemed to me an enchantment.

I remained nonplussed at the sight of her, and, unable to guess the purpose of this visit. I waited, eyes downcast, trembling, for her to explain herself. Her

[20] These tests, conducted at the Sorbonne (then still meaning the Faculty of Theology of the University of Paris), sometimes lasted as long as twelve hours and involved an extremely strenuous defense of a number of propositions against numerous members of the Sorbonne faculty.

embarrassment was for some time equal to mine, but, seeing that my silence continued, she put her hand over her eyes to hide a few tears. She told me, in a timid tone, that she confessed that her infidelity deserved my hatred; but that if it was true that I had ever felt some tenderness for her, there had also been much hardness in my letting two years pass without taking the trouble to inform myself about her lot, and that there still was much in seeing her before me in her present state without saying a word to her. The disorder in my soul as I listened to her cannot be expressed.

She sat down. I remained standing, my body half turned away, not daring to look directly at her. Several times I began a reply that I had not the strength to finish. Finally I made an effort and exclaimed painfully:

"Perfidious Manon! Oh, perfidious, perfidious girl!"

She repeated to me, weeping bitterly, that she did not aim to justify her perfidy.

"What is your aim, then?" I exclaimed.

"I aim to die," she replied, "unless you give me back your heart, without which it is impossible for me to live."

"Then ask for my life, faithless girl!" I went on, myself shedding tears which I tried in vain to restrain. "Ask for my life, which is the only thing I have left to sacrifice to you; for my heart has never ceased to be yours."

Hardly had I finished these words when she rose, transported with joy, and came and embraced me. She smothered me with a thousand passionate caresses. She called me by all the names that love invents to express its most ardent ecstasies. I was still responding only languidly. What a transition, indeed, from the tranquil situation I had been in to the tumultuous impulses that I could feel coming to life again! I was terrified by them. I shuddered, as happens when you find yourself at night in an untraveled countryside: you feel yourself transported into a new order of things; you are seized with a secret horror, from which you recover only after considering all the surroundings for a long time.

We sat down side by side. I took her hands in mine.

"Ah! Manon," I said to her, looking at her sadly, "I had not expected the black treachery with which you repaid my love. It was very easy for you to deceive a heart of which you were absolute sovereign, and which set its whole happiness in pleasing you and obeying you. Now tell me whether you have found any other hearts so tender and submissive. No, no, Nature does not make many of the same temper as mine. Tell me at least whether sometimes you have missed mine. What trust can I place in this return of good feeling that brings you back today to console my heart? I see only too well that you are more charming than ever; but in the name of all the pains I have suffered for you, beautiful Manon, tell me, will you be more faithful?"

She told me in reply such touching things about her repentance, and pledged herself to fidelity by so many vows and protestations, that she softened me to an inexpressible degree.

"Dear Manon!" I said to her in a profane mixture of amorous and theological expressions. "You are too adorable for a created being. I feel my heart carried away by an all-conquering delight. All they say about liberty at Saint-Sulpice is fancy. I am going to lose my fortune and my reputation for you; I foresee it clearly, I read my destiny in your lovely eyes; but for what losses shall I not be consoled by your love! Fortune's favors do not concern me; glory appears as smoke to me; all my plans for an ecclesiastical life were mad imaginings; in short, every good other than what I hope for with you is a good to disdain, since all together they cannot hold out for a moment in my heart against a single one of your glances!"

In promising her nevertheless to forget all her faults, I asked to be informed how she had let herself be led astray by B. . :. She told me that having seen her at her window he had become impassioned for her; he had made his declaration like a true farmer-general, that is to say by notifying her in a letter that the payment would be proportionate to the favors; she had yielded at first, but with no other purpose than to extract from him a considerable sum that could serve to let us live comfortably; he had dazzled her by such magnificent promises that she had let her resolution be shaken by degrees; I should judge her remorse, however, by the grief she had manifested on the eve of our separation. In spite of the opulence in which he had kept her, she had never tasted any happiness with him—not only, she told me, because she found in him nothing of the delicacy of my feelings or the charm of my manners, but because in the very midst of the pleasures that he procured her without end, she bore in the depths of her heart the memory of my love and remorse for her unfaithfulness.

She told me about Tiberge and the extreme confusion that his visit had caused her.

"A sword-thrust in the heart," she added, "would have troubled my blood less. I turned my back on him, unable to bear his presence even for a moment."

She went on to tell me by what means she had been appraised of my stay in Paris, the change in my condition, and my examination at the Sorbonne. She assured me that she had been so agitated during the disputation that she had had much difficulty in restraining not only her tears but even her moans and cries, which more than once had been on the point of bursting forth. Finally, she told me she had left the place last, to hide her emotion, and, following only the impulse of her heart and the impetuosity of her desires, had come straight to the seminary, resolved to die there if she did not find me disposed to forgive her.

Where is the barbarian who would not have been touched by so keen and tender a repentance? As for me, I felt in that moment that I would have sacrificed all the bishoprics in Christendom for Manon. I asked her what new plan she thought appropriate for our affairs. She told me that we must leave the seminary at once and put off making arrangements to some safer place. I consented to all her wishes without question. She entered her carriage and went to wait for me at the street corner. I escaped a short time later without being noticed by the doorkeeper. I got in with her. We went to the secondhand clothing store. I resumed the braided coat and the sword. Manon paid the bills, for I had not a sou; and for fear I might find some obstacle to my leaving Saint-Sulpice, she had opposed my going back to my room for a moment to get my money. My wealth, moreover, was very modest, and she was rich enough from B . . . 's liberalities to despise what she was making me abandon. Even at the clothing store we considered what plan we should adopt. To make me appreciate more fully her sacrificing B . . . to me, she resolved to make no effort to spare him.

"I will leave him his furniture," she said; "it is his; but I shall take, as is only fair, the jewelry and almost sixty thousand francs that I have gotten from him in these two years. I have given him no power over me," she added; "thus we can stay in Paris without fear and take a nice house where we shall live happily."

I pointed out to her that if there was no peril for her, there was much for me, since I could not fail to be recognized sooner or later and I would be continually exposed to the misfortune I had already suffered. She gave me to understand that she would be sorry to leave Paris. I so feared to make her unhappy that there were no risks I would not have despised in order to please her; however, we found a sensible compromise, which was to rent a house in some village in the neighborhood of Paris from which it would be easy for us to go into town whenever pleasure or business called us there. We chose Chail-

lot,[21] which is not far out. Manon went home right
away. I went and waited for her at the little gate
of the Tuileries garden. She came back an hour later
in a hired carriage with a maidservant and a few
trunks in which her clothes and everything precious
she owned were packed.

We were not long in reaching Chaillot. We spent
the first night at the inn to give ourselves time to
look for a house or at least a comfortable apartment. The very next day we found an apartment to
our taste.

At first my happiness seemed unshakably established. Manon was sweetness and complaisance itself. She paid me such delicate attentions that I
thought myself only too perfectly repaid for all my
troubles. Since we had both gained a little experience, we gave some thought to the solidity of our
fortune. Sixty thousand francs, which was the amount
of our funds, was not a sum that could stretch as
far as the course of a long life. Moreover, we were
not disposed to tighten up our expenses too much.
The greatest virtue either of Manon or of me was
not economy. Here is the plan I proposed:

"Sixty thousand francs," I said to her, "can support us for ten years. Two thousand crowns will be
enough for us each year, if we continue to live in
Chaillot. Here we shall lead a comfortable but simple life. Our sole expense will be for the upkeep of
a carriage and for shows. We'll go by rules. You
love the opera: we'll go twice a week. As for gambling,
we'll so limit ourselves that our losses will never ex-
ceed two pistoles.[22] It is impossible that in a period of
ten years there will be no change in my family; my
father is old, he may die. I shall find myself with some
property and then we will be safe from all our other
fears."

[21] Now the part of Paris near the Arc de Triomphe, then
a fashionable suburb.
[22] The 1731 ed. reads "ten pistoles" and (above) allows them
to go to the opera *three* times a week.

This arrangement would not have been the maddest action of my life if we had been disciplined enough to subject ourselves to it constantly; but our resolutions lasted hardly more than a month. Manon was passionate for pleasure; I was passionate for her. There arose at every moment new occasions for expense; and far from regretting the sums that she sometimes used profusely, I was the first to procure her everything I thought likely to please her. Even our residence at Chaillot began to weigh on her. Winter was coming on; everyone was going back to town, and the country was becoming deserted. She proposed that we take a house in Paris again. To this I did not consent; but to satisfy her on one point, I told her that we could rent a furnished apartment in town and spend the night there when we were too late in leaving the gathering we went to several times a week; for the inconvenience of getting back to Chaillot so late was the pretext she offered for wanting to leave there. Thus we allowed ourselves two dwellings, one in town and the other in the country. This change soon brought the ultimate confusion into our affairs by giving rise to two adventures that caused our ruin.

Manon had a brother who was in the Bodyguards.[23] He unfortunately lived on the same street in Paris as we. He recognized his sister, seeing her one morning at her window. He rushed immediately to our apartment. He was a brute with no principles of honor. He came into our room swearing horribly; and since he knew part of his sister's adventures, he overwhelmed her with insults and reproaches. I had gone out a moment before, which was doubtless fortunate either for him or for me, since I had no disposition to put up with an insult. I returned home only after he had left. I could tell by Manon's sadness that something extraordinary had happened. She told me of the unpleasant scene she

---

[23] A cavalry troop originally, but no longer necessarily, composed of noblemen, serving as personal guards to the king.

had just been through and of her brother's brutal threats. I felt so much resentment that I would have run instantly to take vengeance, if she had not stopped me by her tears. While I was discussing this adventure with her, the guardsman came back into the room we were in, without having himself announced. I would not have received him as civilly as I did if I had known him; but, having greeted us with smiles, he had the time to tell Manon that he came to make his excuses for his temper; that he had thought she was living a disorderly life, and this opinion had inflamed his anger; but that having inquired of one of our servants who I was, he had learned such advantageous things about me as to make him wish to live on good terms with us.

Although there was something bizarre and shocking about this information, coming as it did from one of my lackeys, I accepted his compliment civilly. I thought I was pleasing Manon. She seemed charmed to see him inclined to be reconciled. We had him stay to dinner. In a few moments he became so familiar that, having heard us speak of returning to Chaillot, he absolutely insisted on keeping us company. We had to give him a place in our carriage. Thus he took possession; for he soon became so fond of seeing us regularly that he made our house his own and made himself in a sense master of everything that belonged to us. He called me his brother; and, on the pretext of brotherly freedom, he made bold to bring all his friends into our house in Chaillot and entertain them there at our expense. He dressed himself magnificently with our money. He even pledged our names to pay all his debts. I closed my eyes to this tyranny in order not to displease Manon, even to the point of pretending not to notice that he extracted from her, from time to time, considerable sums. It is true that, being a big gambler, he had the good faith to return part of them to her when fortune favored him; but *our* fortune was too slender to meet for long such immoderate expenses.

I was on the point of having a straight talk with him to deliver us from his importunities, when a disastrous incident spared me that trouble while causing us another that ruined us beyond recovery.

One day we had stayed on in Paris overnight, as we very often did. The maidservant, who remained alone in Chaillot on these occasions, came and told me in the morning that a fire had broken out in my house during the night and that it had been put out only with much difficulty. I asked whether our furniture had suffered any damage; she replied that there had been such great confusion, caused by the multitude of strangers who had come to help, that she could not be sure of anything. I trembled for our money, which was locked in a little strongbox. I went promptly to Chaillot. Useless haste: the box had already disappeared.

I then learned that one can love money without being avaricious. This loss pierced me with so sharp a pain that I nearly lost my mind. I suddenly understood to what new woes I was to find myself exposed. Indigence was the least of them. I knew Manon; already I had experienced only too well the fact that, however faithful and attached she was to me in good fortune, she was not to be counted on in misery. She loved abundance and pleasures too well to sacrifice them to me.

"I shall lose her," I exclaimed to myself. "Unhappy Chevalier! So you are again to lose everything you love!"

This thought plunged me into such frightful distress that for a few moments I debated whether I would not do better to end all my woes by death. However, I preserved enough presence of mind to want to examine first whether I had no resource left. Heaven brought to my mind an idea that checked my despair. It came to me that it would not be impossible for me to hide our loss from Manon, and that by ingenuity or by some favorable luck I might provide rather decently for her upkeep so as to prevent her from feeling want.

"I reckoned," I said to myself in consolation, "that twenty thousand crowns would be enough for us for ten years. Suppose the ten years have run out and that none of the changes I hoped for have taken place in my family. What course would I adopt? I hardly know; but what keeps me from doing today what I would do then? How many people live in Paris who have neither my wit nor my natural qualities and who nevertheless owe their support to their talents, such as they are?

"Has not Providence," I added, reflecting on the different conditions of life, "arranged things most wisely? Most of the great nobles and the rich are fools: that is clear to anyone who knows anything of the world. Now there is an admirable justice in that: if they combined wit with riches, they would be too fortunate, and the rest of mankind too wretched. To the latter are granted the qualities of body and soul, as means to draw them out of misery and poverty. Some take a share of the riches of the great by serving their pleasures: they make them their dupes. Others serve their instruction: they try to make good men of them. To tell the truth, it is rare that they succeed; but that is not the aim of the divine wisdom: they always reap some fruit from their cares, which is that of living at the expense of those whom they instruct; and however you take it, an excellent source of revenue to the little people is the stupidity of the rich and the great."

These thoughts set me up a bit in heart and head. I resolved first to consult Monsieur Lescaut, Manon's brother. He knew Paris perfectly, and I had had only too many chances to learn that it was neither from his own funds nor from the king's pay that he derived his most obvious source of revenue. I had barely twenty pistoles left, which fortunately had happened to be in my pocket. I showed him my purse, explaining to him my misfortune and my fears, and asked him whether I had a course to choose between those of dying of hunger and blowing my brains out from despair. He replied that blowing your brains out was the expedient of idiots; that as for dying of hunger, there were plenty of intelligent people who found themselves reduced to it when they would not make use of their talents; that it was up to me to examine what I was capable of; that he assured me of his help and advice in anything I might undertake.

"That is very vague, Monsieur Lescaut," I said to him; "my needs crave a more immediate remedy; for what do you expect me to say to Manon?"

"Apropos of Manon," he retorted, "what is worrying you? Don't you always have in her all you need to end your worries whenever you want? A girl like her should support us all, you, herself, and me."

He cut short the reply that this impertinence deserved from me and went on to tell me that he guaranteed me a thousand crowns to share among us before evening, if I was willing to follow his advice; that he knew a nobleman so liberal in the matter of pleasures that he was sure that a thousand crowns would be nothing to him to obtain the favors of[24] a girl like Manon. I stopped him.

"I had a better opinion of you," I told him in reply; "I had supposed that the motive you had for granting me your friendship was a very different feeling from the one you have now."

He confessed to me shamelessly that he had always thought the same way and that once his sister had violated the laws of her sex, although in favor of the man he liked best, he had become reconciled with her only in hope of deriving some profit from her bad conduct. It was easy for me to judge that until then we had been his dupes. Nevertheless, in spite of my reaction to this statement, my need of him obliged me to reply, laughing, that his advice

[24] 1731 ed.: "to spend the night with."

was a last resort that I must put off to the final extremity. I begged him to open up some other way to me.

He proposed to me to profit by my youth and the good looks I had received from nature to establish relations with some generous old lady. I had no liking for this plan either, which would have made me unfaithful to Manon. I spoke to him about gambling as the easiest way and the one most suitable to my situation. He told me that gambling was indeed a resource, but that it needed to be explained; that to undertake simply to gamble, with the ordinary hopes, was the real way to complete my ruin; that to hope to practice alone, without support, the little methods that an able man employs to correct fortune was too dangerous a trade; that there was a third course, which was that of joint action, but that my youth made him fear that the associates might judge that I did not yet have the qualities fit for the league. Nevertheless, he promised to use his good offices with them; and, what I would not have expected from him, he offered me some money whenever I should find myself pressed by need. The only favor I asked of him in the circumstances was not to let Manon know anything about the loss I had undergone and the subject of our conversation.

I left his place even less satisfied than when I went in. I even repented of having confided my secret to him. He had done nothing for me that I could not have obtained just as well without this disclosure; and I was mortally afraid that he might break his promise to reveal nothing to Manon. I also had reason to apprehend, from his declaration of his feelings, that he might form the plan of deriving some profit from her (to use his own terms) by taking her out of my hands, or at least by advising her to leave me and attach herself to some richer and more fortunate lover. A thousand things occurred to me on that score, whose only result was to torment me and renew the despair I had been in that morning. It came to my mind several times to write to my father and feign a new conversion to obtain some monetary aid from him; but I remembered immediately that in spite of all his kindness, he had shut me up for six months in a tight prison for my first mistake; I was quite sure that, for such a sensation as my flight from Saint-Sulpice must have caused, he would treat me much more rigorously. Finally this welter of thoughts produced one which all at once restored calm to my mind and which I was astonished not to have had earlier. This was to turn again to my friend Tiberge, in whom I was quite certain always to find the same fund of zeal and friendship.

Nothing is more admirable or does more honor to virtue than the confidence with which we approach people whose probity we know perfectly. We feel that there is no risk to be run. If they are not always in a position to offer help, we are sure we will at least obtain kindness and compassion. The heart, which closes so carefully to the rest of mankind, opens naturally in their presence, as a flower blossoms out in the light of the sun, from which it expects only a gentle influence.

I considered it an effect of Heaven's protection to have remembered Tiberge at such an appropriate time, and I resolved to find a way to see him before the day was over. I went back home immediately to write him a line and set a suitable place for our talk. I recommended silence and discretion as one of the most important favors he could do me in the state of my affairs. The joy I felt at the hope of seeing him wiped out the traces of chagrin that Manon would not have failed to perceive upon my face. I told her of our Chaillot mishap as of a trifle that should not alarm her; and, Paris being the place in the world where she took the most pleasure to be, she was not sorry to hear me say that it would be a good thing for us to stay there until they had repaired some slight effects of the fire in Chaillot. An

hour later I received my answer from Tiberge, who
promised to be at the appointed place. I hurried
there impatiently. Nevertheless, I felt some shame at
going to appear before the eyes of a friend whose
mere presence should be a reproach to my disorders;
but the opinion I had of the goodness of his heart,
and Manon's interest, sustained my boldness.

I had asked him to be in the garden of the Pal-
ais-Royal. He was there before me. He came and
embraced me as soon as he saw me. For a long
time he held me clasped in his arms, and I felt my
face wet with his tears. I told him that it was only
with confusion that I came to see him, and that I
bore in my heart a keen sense of my ingratitude;
that the first thing I implored of him was to let me
know whether I was still allowed to regard him as
my friend, after having so justly deserved to lose his
esteem and affection. He replied in the tenderest
tone that nothing could make him renounce that title; that my very misfortunes, and, if he might be
allowed to say so, my errors and disorders, had
doubled his tenderness toward me; but that this was
a tenderness mixed with the keenest sorrow, such
as we feel for someone dear to us whom we see
on the brink of disaster without being able to help
him.

We sat down on a bench.

"Alas!" I said to him, sighing from the depths of
my heart. "Your compassion must be extraordinary,
my dear Tiberge, if you assure me it is equal to my
woes. I am ashamed to let you see them, for I confess their cause is not glorious; but their effect is so
sad that a person need not love me as much as
you do in order to be touched."

He asked me, as a sign of friendship, to tell him
without dissimulation what had happened to me since
I left Saint-Sulpice. I satisfied him, and far from al-
tering the truth in any matter or minimizing my errors to make them appear more excusable, I told
him of my passion with all the vigor it inspired in

me. I represented it to him as one of those peculiar blows, of a destiny that applies itself to ruining a poor wretch, which it is as impossible for virtue to repel as it was for wisdom to foresee. I painted a vivid picture of my agitations, my fears, the despair I was in two hours before seeing him and into which I would fall back, if I were abandoned by my friends as pitilessly as by fortune; in short, I so touched the kind Tiberge that I saw he was as afflicted by compassion as I was by the feeling of my woes. He never tired of embracing me and exhorting me to take courage and comfort; but since he was still assuming that I had to part with Manon, I gave him to understand that it was this very separation that I regarded as the greatest of my misfortunes, and that I was ready to suffer not only the last extremity of misery but the cruelest of deaths before accepting a remedy more unbearable than all my woes together.

"Then explain yourself," he said to me: "what sort of help am I able to give you, if you rebel against everything I propose?"

I did not dare declare to him that it was his purse I needed. However, he finally understood it; and, having acknowledged that he thought he followed me, he remained for some time hesitant, with the air of a person in doubt.

"Do not think," he soon went on, "that my reverie comes from a cooling of zeal and friendship. But to what an alternative are you reducing me, if I must refuse the only assistance you are willing to accept, or violate my duty by granting it? For is it not taking part in your licentiousness to help you persevere in it? However," he continued after reflecting for a moment, "I imagine that it is perhaps the violent state into which indigence casts you that does not leave you enough freedom to choose the best course; we need a tranquil mind to enjoy wisdom and truth. I'll find a way to let you have some money. Allow me, my dear Chevalier," he added, embracing me, "to set only one condition, that you will let me know the place where you are living and allow me at least to do what I can to bring you back to virtue, which I know you love, and from which only the violence of your passions makes you stray."

I sincerely granted him all he wished and begged him to deplore the malignity of my lot, which made me profit so poorly by the counsels of so virtuous a friend. He immediately took me to a banker he knew, who advanced me a hundred pistoles against his note, for he was low in ready cash. I have already said that he was not rich. His benefice was worth a thousand crowns yearly, but since this was the first year he had it, he had as yet got none of the revenue: it was on his future income that he was making me this advance.

I felt the full value of his generosity. I was touched by it, to the point of deploring the blindness of a fatal love that made me violate all duties. Virtue had enough strength, for a few moments, to rise up in my heart against my passion, and I at least perceived, in that moment of enlightenment, the shame and indignity of my chains. But this combat was light and did not last. The sight of Manon would have made me plunge headlong from Heaven; and I was astounded, when I was back with her, that I could for a moment have considered as shameful so just a tenderness for so charming a person.

Manon was a creature with an extraordinary character. Never was a girl less attached to money than she; but she could not be at ease for a moment when in fear of lacking it. It was pleasure and pastimes that she needed. She would never have wanted to touch a sou if entertainment had cost nothing. She never even inquired about the condition of our resources, provided she could spend the day pleasantly; so that being neither excessively addicted to gambling nor able to be dazzled by the splendor of great expenditures, nothing was easier than to satisfy her by daily creating amusements that were to her taste.

But it was so necessary a thing for her to be thus occupied by pleasure that without this one could not rely in the least on her temperament and her inclinations. Although she loved me tenderly and I was the only one, as she readily admitted, who could give her perfect enjoyment of the sweets of love, I was almost certain that her affection would not stand up against certain fears. She would have preferred me to the whole world, with a modest fortune; but I had no doubt whatever that she would abandon me for some new B . . . when I had nothing left but constancy and fidelity to offer her.

So I resolved to regulate my personal expenditure so well as to be always in a position to provide for hers, and rather to deprive myself of a thousand necessities than to limit her even in superfluities. The carriage frightened me more than all the rest; for there seemed no likelihood that I could maintain horses and a coachman.

I revealed my problem to Monsieur Lescaut. I had not concealed from him the fact that I had received a hundred pistoles from a friend. He told me again that if I wanted to try the hazards of gambling, he was not without hope that on cheerfully sacrificing some hundred francs to entertain his associates, I might be admitted, on his recommendation, to the Ligue de l'Industrie.[25] For all my repugnance to cheating, I let myself be drawn in by cruel necessity.

Monsieur Lescaut introduced me, that very evening, as a relative of his. He added that I was all the more likely to succeed because I was in need of fortune's greatest favors. However, to make it known that my indigence was not that of a nobody, he said that I was minded to treat them to supper. The offer was accepted. I entertained them magnificently. There was much talk of the fine figure I cut and of my promising aptitudes. They claimed that much

[25] The League of Industry or of Ingenuity; in fact, as will be seen, an association of card sharps.

could be hoped for me because there was something in my face that bespoke the gentleman, and no one would suspect my artifices. Finally they offered a vote of thanks to Monsieur Lescaut for having recruited a novice of my merit for the Order, and appointed one of the knights to spend a few days giving me the necessary instructions.

The principal theater of my exploits was to be the Hôtel de Transylvanie,[26] where there was a faro table in one room and various other card and dice games in the gallery. This academy was run for the profit of the prince de R . . . , who was then living at Clagny, and most of his officers belonged to our society. Shall I say it to my shame?[27] In a short time I profited from my master's lessons. I acquired an especially great facility in turning cards over and in recognizing them by their backs; and with the very great help of a long pair of sleeves, I could conjure a card away deftly enough to deceive the eyes of the sharpest and quite naturally to ruin many honest gamblers. This extraordinary skill so hastened the progress of my fortune that in a few weeks I owned considerable sums, besides those that I shared in good faith with my associates. No longer did I then fear to reveal to Manon our loss at Chaillot; and to console her, when I broke the sad news to her, I rented a furnished house, where we established ourselves with every appearance of opulence and security.

Tiberge had not failed, during this time, to pay me frequent visits. His moralizing never ended. He constantly began anew to point out to me the wrong I was doing to my conscience, my honor, and my fortune. I received his advice as a friend; and although I had not the slightest inclination to follow it, I was grateful to him for his zeal, because I knew its source. Sometimes I teased him good-humoredly in

26 The residence of Francis Rákóczy, prince of Transylvania, a refugee in Paris after his revolt against Austria, who, needing money, made the place a gambling house.

27 This sentence does not appear in the 1731 edition.

the very presence of Manon, and exhorted him not to be more scrupulous than a large number of bishops and other priests,[28] who very well knew how to reconcile a mistress and a benefice.

"Look," I would say to him, showing him my own mistress' eyes, "and tell me whether there are faults that are not justified by so beautiful a cause."

He took patience. He even pushed it rather far; but when he saw that my riches were increasing, and that I not only had returned his hundred pistoles to him, but, having rented a new house and doubled my expense, was about to plunge back deeper than ever into pleasures, he changed his tone and manners entirely. He complained that I had grown hardened; he threatened me with chastisement from Heaven, and predicted to me part of the misfortunes that wasted little time in happening to me.

"It is impossible," he said to me, "that the riches which serve to support your dissipation have come to you by legitimate ways. You have acquired them unjustly; they will be snatched away from you in the same way. God's most terrible punishment would be to let you enjoy them undisturbed. All my advice," he added, "has been useless to you; I foresee only too well that it will soon be importunate. Farewell, weak and ungrateful friend. May your criminal pleasures vanish like a shadow! May your fortune and your money perish without resource, and may you remain naked and alone, to feel the vanity of the goods that have intoxicated you so madly! It is then that you will find me ready to love you and serve you; but today I break off all dealings with you, and I detest the life you lead."

It was in my room and before Manon's eyes that he served me with this apostolic harangue. He got up to leave. I started to detain him, but I was stopped by Manon, who told me he was a madman and that we should let him go.

[28] 1731 ed.: "than most bishops and other priests."

His speech did not fail to make some impression on me. I note in this way the various occasions on which my heart felt a turning back toward the good; because it was to that recollection that I later owed a part of my strength in the unhappiest circumstances of my life.

Manon's caresses dissipated in a moment the chagrin that this scene had caused me. We continued to lead a life made up entirely of pleasure and love. The increase of our riches redoubled our affection. Venus and Fortune had no happier and more tender slaves. Heavens! Why call this world a vale of tears, since here one can enjoy such charming delights! But alas! Their weakness is that they pass too quickly. What other felicity would anyone aim at, if they were of a nature to last forever? Ours shared the common lot, that is to say they did not long endure and were followed by bitter regrets.

I had compiled such considerable winnings at gambling that I was thinking of investing part of my money. My servants were not unaware of my successes, especially my valet and Manon's maid, in front of whom we often talked in all confidence. This girl was pretty. My valet was in love with her. They were dealing with easy young masters, whom they supposed they could easily deceive. They made a plan to do so, and executed it with such unhappy results for us that they put us into a state from which it was never possible for us to rise again.

Monsieur Lescaut having had us one day to supper, it was about midnight when we returned home. I called my valet, and Manon her maid; neither one appeared. We were told that they had not been seen in the house since eight o'clock, and that they had gone out after having some cases taken away, according to orders which they said they had received from me. I sensed part of the truth; but I formed no suspicions that were not surpassed by what I perceived on entering my room. The lock on my closet had been forced, and my money taken with all

my clothes. While I was reflecting, alone, on this disaster, Manon came along in a fright to tell me that
the same damage had been done in her room. The
blow seemed to be so cruel that it was only an extraordinary effort of my reason that kept me from
giving in to cries and tears. The fear of communicating my despair to Manon made me put on a show
of calm. I told her jokingly that I would avenge myself on some dupe at the Hôtel de Transylvanie. However, she seemed to me so affected by our misfortune
that her sadness had much more power to distress
me than my feigned good spirits had had to keep
her from being too downcast.

"We are lost!" she said to me, with tears in her
eyes.

I tried in vain to console her by my caresses. My
own tears betrayed my consternation and despair. In
fact, we were so absolutely ruined that we had not
a stitch left.

I decided to send right away for Monsieur Lescaut.
He advised me to go that very instant to see the
Lieutenant General of Police and the Grand Provost
of Paris.[29] I went, but only to my greater undoing; for
besides the fact that this step, and those that I got
these two officers of justice to take, produced nothing, I gave Lescaut time to talk to his sister and inspire in her, in my absence, a horrible resolution.
He told her about Monsieur de G . . . M . . . , an old
voluptuary who paid prodigally for his pleasures, and
he brought her to see so many advantages in putting
herself on his payroll that, upset as she was by our
disaster, she agreed to everything he undertook to
persuade her of. This honorable bargain was concluded before I came back and the execution of it put
off to the next day, after Lescaut had notified Monsieur de G . . . M . . . .

I found him waiting for me at home; but Manon
had gone to bed in her room and given orders to

[29] The chiefs of the Paris police and of the Paris judiciary.

her lackey to tell me that needing a little rest, she asked me to leave her alone that night. Lescaut left me, after offering me a few pistoles, which I accepted. It was almost four o'clock when I went to bed; and, being then still long occupied with ways to restore my fortunes, I went to sleep so late that I could not wake up until eleven or twelve. I got up promptly to go and ask how Manon was; I was told that she had gone out an hour before with her brother, who had come to get her in a hired cab. Although such a move, made with Lescaut, seemed mysterious to me, I made a violent effort and held back my suspicions. I let a few hours slip by, which I spent reading. Finally, no longer master of my uneasiness, I paced through our rooms. In Manon's I perceived a sealed letter on her table. It was addressed to me, and the handwriting was hers. I opened it with a deathly shiver: it was in these words:

> I swear to you, my dear Chevalier, that you are the idol of my heart, and that there is no one but you in the world whom I can love as I love you; but don't you see, my poor dear heart, that in the condition to which we are reduced, fidelity is a stupid virtue? Do you think one can be very tender when one has no bread? Hunger would lead me into some fatal mistake; one day I would utter my last sigh thinking it was a sigh of love. I adore you, count on that; but for a little while, leave the management of our fortune to me. Woe to him who falls into my nets! I am working to make my Chevalier rich and happy. My brother will tell you the news of your Manon, and that she wept at the need to leave you.

After reading this I remained in a state that would be hard for me to describe; for I do not know even today by what sort of feelings I was then agitated. It was one of those unique situations the like of which one has never experienced: one cannot possibly explain them to others, because they have no idea of them; and one has difficulty in unraveling them adequately to oneself, because, being the only ones of their kind, they are not linked to anything in our memory and cannot even be related to any known feeling. However, whatever was the nature of mine, it is certain that their ingredients must have included sorrow, spite, jealousy, and shame. I would have been fortunate if love had not been the main one.

"She loves me, that I *will* believe," I exclaimed; "but would she not have to be a monster in order to hate me? What rights did anyone ever have over another's heart that I do not have over hers? What is there left for me to do for her, after all I have sacrificed to her? Yet she abandons me! And the ingrate thinks to shelter herself from my reproaches by telling me that she has not stopped loving me. She dreads hunger. God of Love! What coarseness of feeling! And what a bad response to my delicacy! I did not dread it, I who expose myself to it so willingly by giving up my fortune and the comforts of my father's house, I who have cut out even necessities of my own so as to satisfy her little whims and caprices. She adores me, she says. If you adored me, ungrateful girl, I know very well whose advice you would have taken; you would at least not have left me without saying good-by. I am the one who can say what cruel pains one feels on being separated from the person one adores. To expose oneself to these pains voluntarily, one must have lost one's mind."

My laments were interrupted by a visit I was not expecting. It was from Lescaut.

"Hangman!" I said to him, putting my hand to my sword. "Where is Manon? What have you done with her?"

This movement frightened him; he answered that if that was how I greeted him when he was coming to give me an account of the most important favor he could possibly have done me, he would take his leave and never again set foot in my house. I ran to the door of my room and shut it carefully.

"Do not imagine," I said, turning to him, "that you can once again make a dupe of me and deceive me with your tales. You must either defend your life, or see that I find Manon."

"My word! How impetuous you are!" he replied. "That is the only thing that brings me here. I come to announce a piece of good fortune which you aren't expecting and for which you perhaps will recognize that you are somewhat in my debt."

I insisted on being enlightened at once. He told me that Manon, unable to endure the fear of want and especially the idea of being obliged suddenly to cut down our way of living, had asked him to arrange for her to meet Monsieur de G . . . M . . . , who was considered a generous man. He was careful not to tell me that this counsel had come from him or that he had prepared the way before he took her there.

"I brought her there this morning," he went on, "and that gentleman was so delighted with her merit that he first invited her to keep him company in his country house, where he has gone to spend a few days. As for me," added Lescaut, "since I saw all at once how advantageous that could be for you, I adroitly gave him to understand that Manon had suffered some considerable losses, and I so spurred his generosity that he began by making her a present of two hundred pistoles. I told him that that was nice for the present, but that the future would bring great demands on my sister; that moreover she had taken on the care of a young brother, who had been left on our hands after the death of our father and mother, and that if he thought her worthy of his esteem, he would not let her suffer in the person of this young child, whom she regarded as part of herself. This story did not fail to touch him. He has undertaken to rent a comfortable house for you and Manon, for it is you yourself who are this poor little orphan brother. He has promised to furnish your house nicely

and to supply you every month with a good four hundred livres, which will make, if I am counting right,
four thousand eight hundred at the end of each year.
He left orders with his steward, before leaving for his
country estate, to look for a house and hold it ready for
his return. Then you will again see Manon, who told
me to embrace you a thousand times for her and to
assure you that she loves you more than ever."

I sat down and mused about this bizarre arrangement of my lot. I found myself with divided feelings,
and consequently in a state of uncertainty so hard
to terminate that I remained for a long time without
reply to a quantity of questions that Lescaut asked
me one on top of the other. It was in that moment
that honor and virtue made me feel again the stings
of remorse and that I cast my eyes, sighing, toward
Amiens, my father's house, Saint-Sulpice, and all the
places where I had lived in innocence. By what an
immense space I was separated from that happy state!
I could no longer see it except from a distance, like a
shadow which still attracted my regrets and desires
but was too weak to incite me to any efforts.

"By what fatality," I said to myself, "have I become so criminal? Love is an innnocent passion; how
has it changed for me into a source of miseries and
disorders? Who kept me from living a tranquil and
virtuous life with Manon? Why didn't I marry her
before obtaining anything from her love? Wouldn't
my father, who loved me so tenderly, have consented
to it if I had pressed him to with legitimate entreaties? Ah! My father would have cherished her himself as a charming girl only too worthy to be his
son's wife; I would be happy with Manon's love, with
my father's affection, with decent people's esteem,
with the bounties of fortune, and the tranquillity of
virtue. Disastrous reversal! What infamous role is this
that is now proposed for me to play? What, I should
share . . . But is it possible to hesitate, if it is Manon
who arranged it, and if without this complaisance I
lose her?"

"Monsieur Lescaut," I exclaimed, closing my eyes as if to push away such painful reflections, "if you intended to do me a service, I give you thanks. You might have chosen a more decent way; but that's over and done with, isn't it? So let's not think about anything any more but profiting by your solicitude and fulfilling your plan."

Lescaut, who had been embarrassed by my anger, followed by a very long silence, was delighted to see me take a very different position from the one he had no doubt feared; he was anything but brave, and I had better proofs of this later on.

"Yes, yes," he hastened to answer, "I have done you a very good service, and you'll see that we'll get more advantage out of it than you think."

We agreed on the way we could anticipate the suspicions that Monsieur de G . . . M . . . might entertain about our being brothers when he saw that I was bigger and perhaps a little older than he imagined. We found no other way than for me to assume in his presence a simple, provincial manner, and to make him believe that I was planning to enter Church orders and that for this reason I was going to school every day. We also resolved that I should dress very badly the first time that I should be allowed the honor of meeting him.

He came back to town three or four days later; he himself brought Manon to the house that his steward had taken care to prepare. She immediately notified Lescaut of her return; and, he having informed me, we both went to her place. The old beau had already left.

In spite of the resignation with which I had submitted to her wishes, I could not suppress the murmurings of my heart when I saw her. I appeared to her sad and languishing. The joy of finding her again did not win out completely over the chagrin at her infidelity. She, on the contrary, appeared transported with the pleasure of seeing me again. She reproached me for my coldness. I could not keep from uttering the words "perfidious" and "faithless," which I accompanied with as many sighs. At first she made fun of me for my simplicity; but when she saw my eyes still fixed sadly on her, and the pain it cost me to digest a change so contrary to my character and my desires, she went alone into her boudoir. I followed her a moment later. I found her there all in tears. I asked her what caused them.

"That is very easy for you to see," she said to me. "How can you expect me to live, if the sight of me is now fit only to make you look somber and gloomy? You have not given me one caress in a whole hour that you have been here, and you have accepted mine with the majesty of the Grand Turk in his harem."

"Listen, Manon," I said, embracing her, "I cannot conceal from you that my heart is deathly distressed. I am not now speaking of the alarms that your unexpected flight caused me, nor of the cruelty you showed me in abandoning me without one word of consolation, after spending the night in another bed than mine. The charm of your presence would make me forget much more. But do you believe that I can think without sighs, and even without tears," I continued, shedding some, "of the sad and unhappy life that you want me to lead in this house? Let's leave aside my birth and my honor: it is no longer such feeble reasons that should come into competition with a love such as mine; but that love itself, don't you suppose that it is moaning to see itself so ill rewarded, or rather so cruelly treated, by an ungrateful and harsh mistress?"

She interrupted me.

"Look here, my own Chevalier," she said, "it is useless to torment me by reproaches, which pierce my heart when they come from you. I see what wounds you. I had hoped that you would consent to the plan I had made to restore our fortune a bit, and it was out of concern for your delicacy that I had begun to carry it out without your participation; but I give it up, since you do not approve."

She added that she asked of me only a little indulgence for the rest of the day; that she had already received two hundred pistoles from her aged lover, and that he had promised to bring her that evening a beautiful pearl necklace and some other jewels, and, on top of that, half of the annual pension he had promised her.

"Just leave me time enough," she said to me, "to receive his presents; I swear to you he will not be able to boast of any advantages I have given him over me,[30] for I have put him off thus far until we should be in town. It is true that he has kissed my hands a million times and more; it is just that he should pay for this pleasure, and five or six thousand francs will not be too much, as a price proportionate to his riches and his age."

Her resolution pleased me much more than the hope of the five thousand livres. I had occasion to recognize that my heart had not yet lost all feeling of honor, since it was so satisfied to escape infamy. But I was born for brief joys and long sorrows. Fortune delivered me from one abyss only to plunge me into another. When I had shown Manon, by a thousand caresses, how happy I thought myself for her change of plan, I told her that Monsieur Lescaut must be informed of it, so that our measures should be taken concertedly. He murmured about it at first; but the four or five thousand livres in cash made him come gaily around to our views. So it was settled that we should all come to supper with Monsieur de G. . . . M . . . , and this for two reasons: one, to give us the pleasure of an agreeable scene in passing me off as a schoolboy, brother of Manon; the other, to keep the old libertine from making too free with my mistress because of the rights he would think he had

---

[30] 1731 ed. "he will not have the satisfaction of having spent a single night with me."

acquired by paying so liberally in advance. We were to retire, Lescaut and I, when he went up to the room in which he intended to spend the night, and Manon, instead of following him, promised us to leave and come and spend it with me. Lescaut undertook to have a carriage at the door at the right moment.

Time for supper having come, Monsieur de G... M... did not keep us waiting long. Lescaut was in the room with his sister The old man's first compliment was to offer his beauty a necklace, some bracelets, and some earrings, all of pearls and worth at least a thousand crowns. He then counted out to her, in fine louis d'or, the sum of two thousand four hundred livres, which was half her year's pension. He seasoned his present with quantities of sweet phrases in the taste of the old-time court. Manon could not refuse him a few kisses; they were so many rights that she thus acquired to the money he was putting into her hands. I was at the door, where I lent an ear, while waiting for Lescaut to tell me to come in.

He came and took me by the hand, when Manon lad locked up the money and the jewels, and, leading me up to Monsieur de G... M..., he ordered me to make my bow. I made two or three of the deepest.

"Excuse him, sir," said Lescaut to him, "he is a very inexperienced child. He is far indeed, as you see, from having Parisian manners, but we hope that a little practice will form him. You will have the honor of seeing this gentleman here often," he added, turning toward me; "take full advantage of so good a model."

The old lover seemed to take pleasure in seeing me. He gave me two or three little taps on the cheek, telling me that I was a nice-looking boy, but that I would have to be on my guard in Paris, where young people let themselves lapse easily into debauchery. Lescaut assured him that I was naturally so well-behaved that I talked of nothing but becoming a priest, and that my greatest pleasure was in doing the rounds of the little chapels.[31]

"I think he is much like Manon," the old man went on, raising my chin with his hand. I answered naïvely:

"Sir, that is because we are closely connected in the flesh, and thus I love my sister Manon like another self."

"Do you hear him?" he said to Lescaut. "He has wit. It's a pity that child hasn't been around more with people of society."

"Oh, sir," I went on, "I've seen lots of them back home in the churches. and I do believe I'll find some of them in Paris that are bigger fools than I."

"See!" he added. "That's admirable for a country boy."

All our conversation during supper was in about the same taste. Manon, who loved a joke, was several times on the point of spoiling everything by her bursts of laughter. I found occasion as I ate to tell him his own story and the unpleasant fate that threatened him. Lescaut and Manon trembled during my account, especially when I was painting his portrait to the life; but his vanity kept him from recognizing himself in it, and I finished it so adroitly that he was the first to find it very laughable. You will see that I have had my reasons for enlarging on this ridiculous scene.

Finally, when it came time for sleep, he spoke of love and impatience.[32] Lescaut and I withdrew; he was shown to his room; and Manon, having stepped out on the pretext of some need, came and joined us at the door. The carriage, which was waiting for us three or four houses down, came on to pick us up. In a moment we moved far from that part of town.

[31] The French expression here, *faire de petites chapelles*, has two overt pious meanings—the one given above and that of actually building little toy chapels—and another colloquial derivative one, that of belonging to a clique or society such as the League of Ingenuity (pp. 66-67 above). It may be meant here in any of these senses.

[32] 1731 ed.: "he proposed to Manon that they go to bed."

Although in my own eyes this action was a real piece of rascality, it was not the most unjust one that I thought I had to reproach myself with. I had more scruples about the money I had acquired in gambling. However, we profited as little by the one as by the other, and Heaven allowed the lesser of these two injustices to be the more rigorously punished.

Monsieur de G . . . M . . . did not take long to perceive that he was duped. I do not know whether he took, that very evening, some steps to find us; but he had enough influence for these steps not to be long ineffective, while we were imprudent enough to count too heavily on the size of Paris and the distance between our quarter and his. Not only was he soon informed of our address and our present circumstances, but he also learned who I was, the life I had lived in Paris, Manon's old liaison with B . . . , the trick she had played on him—in a word, all the scandalous parts of our story. He thereupon resolved to have us arrested and to treat us less as criminals than as out-and-out debauchees. We were still in bed when a police officer came into our bedroom with a half dozen guards. They first seized our money, or rather Monsieur de G . . . M . . . 's; and having made us get up abruptly, they took us to the door, where we found two coaches, in one of which poor Manon was carried off without explanation, and I dragged away in the other to Saint-Lazare.[33]

One must have suffered such calamities to judge the despair they can cause. Our guards were so harsh as not to allow me to embrace Manon or say a word to her. I did not know for a long time what had become of her. It was no doubt fortunate for me not to have known it at first; for such a terrible catastrophe would have made me lose my senses, and perhaps my life.

So my unhappy mistress was carried off before my

[33] Headquarters of the religious Congrégation de la Mission, located in the Faubourg Saint-Denis, where errant young men of quality were sometimes sent to reform their ways.

eyes and taken to a retreat too horrible to name.
What a fate for an utterly charming creature, who
would have occupied the highest throne in the world
if all men had had my eyes and my heart! She
was not treated barbarically there, but she was locked
up in a small prison cell, alone, and condemned to
complete a certain amount of work every day as a
necessary condition for obtaining some disgusting
food. I learned this sad detail only a long time after,
when I myself had suffered several months of harsh
and tedious penance. Since my guards had also not
informed me of the place where they had orders to
take me, I learned my destiny only at the gates of
Saint-Lazare. I would have preferred death, at that
moment, to the state into which I thought I was
about to fall. I had terrible ideas about this institution. My fear increased when, on entrance, the
guards searched my pockets a second time to make
sure I still had neither weapons nor means of defense. The Superior appeared at once; he had been
notified of my arrival. He greeted me with great
mildness.

"Father," I said, "no indignities. I will die a thousand deaths rather than suffer even one."

"No, no, sir," he replied, "you will behave well,
and we shall be well pleased with one another."

He asked me to come up to an upper room. I
followed him without resistance. The archers accompanied us to the door, and the Superior, having come
in with me, signaled them to go.

"So I am your prisoner!" I said to him. "Well,
Father, what do you intend to do with me?"

He told me that he was delighted to see me adopt
a reasonable tone; that it would be his duty to strive
to inspire in me a taste for virtue and religion, and
mine to profit by his exhortations and advice; that if
I would respond even a little to his efforts on my
behalf, I would find nothing but pleasure in my solitude.

"Ah, pleasure!" I retorted. "Father, you do not

know the only thing that is capable of giving me
any!"

"I know it," he answered, "but I hope that your
inclination will change."

His reply made me understand that he was informed of my adventures, and perhaps of my name.
I asked him to enlighten me. He told me quite naturally that he had been told about everything.

Learning this was the harshest of all my punishments. I shed a torrent of tears and showed every
sign of frightful despair. I could not console myself
for a humiliation that would make me the talk of
everyone I knew and the shame of my family. I
spent a week thus in the deepest dejection, unable
to understand anything or to occupy my mind with
anything but my opprobrium. Even the remembrance
of Manon added nothing to my grief. At least it came
into it only as a feeling that had preceded this new
misery; and the dominant passion in my soul was shame
and confusion.

There are few people who know the power of
these special workings of the heart. The ordinary run
of men are susceptible to only five or six passions, in
the circle of which their lives pass, and to which all
their agitations are limited. Take from them love
and hate, pleasure and pain, hope and fear, and they
feel nothing any more. But persons of a nobler character[34] may be tossed about in a thousand different
ways; it seems as though they have more than five
senses and are accessible to ideas and sensations that
go beyond the ordinary limits of nature. And since
they have a sense of this greatness that raises them
above the common herd, there is nothing of which they
are more jealous. Thence it comes about that they suffer
scorn and ridicule so impatiently, and that shame is one
of their most violent passions.

I had this sad advantage at Saint-Lazare. My sadness seemed so excessive to the Superior that, appre-

[34] 1731 ed.: "of a certain character."

hending its consequences, he thought he must treat me with much kindness and indulgence. He used to visit me two or three times a day. He often took me with him for a walk around the garden, and lavished his zeal in exhortations and salutary advice. I received this gently. I even showed gratitude to him. From this he derived hope for my conversion.

"You have such a gentle and amiable nature," he said to me one day, "that I cannot understand the excesses of which you are accused. Two things astound me: one, how with such good qualities you could abandon yourself to this extreme of debauchery; and the other, which I marvel at even more, how you so willingly accept my advice and instructions after living several years in the habit of vice. If this is repentance, you are a signal example of the mercies of Heaven; if it is natural goodness, you have at least an excellent basic character, which makes me hope that we shall not need to detain you here long in order to bring you back to a decent and regulated life."

I was delighted to see that he had this opinion of me. I resolved to confirm it by behavior that could satisfy him completely, convinced that this was the surest way to shorten my imprisonment. I asked him for books. He was surprised that when he left me the choice of those that I wanted to read I decided on a few serious authors.[35] I pretended to apply myself to study with the utmost assiduity, and thus I gave him, on every occasion, proofs of the change he wished for.

However, this was only external. I must confess it to my shame, I played a hypocrite's role at Saint-Lazare. Instead of studying, when I was alone, I did nothing but bemoan my destiny. I cursed my prison and the tyranny that detained me there. I no sooner had some relief from the dejection into which my humiliation had cast me than I fell back into the torments of love. The absence of Manon, the uncertain-

[35] 1731 ed.: "serious Christian authors."

ty over her fate, the fear of never seeing her again,
were the sole subject of my sad meditations. I pic-
tured her in the arms of G . . . M . . ., for that is the
thought I had had at first; and far from imagining that
he had dealt her the same treatment as to me, I was
persuaded that he had had me sent away only in order to possess her in peace.

Thus I spent days and nights whose length seemed
to me eternal. I had no hope except in the success
of my hypocrisy. I carefully observed the Superior's
face and remarks in order to make sure what he
thought of me; and I made it my study to please him,
as the arbiter of my destiny. It was easy for me to
recognize that I was entirely in his good graces. I no
longer doubted that he would be disposed to do me
service.

One day I made bold to ask him whether it was
on him that my release depended. He told me that
his powers over that were not absolute, but that on
his testimony he hoped that Monsieur de G . . .
M . . ., on whose solicitation the Lieutenant General of Police had had me locked up, would consent
to restore me my freedom.

"May I flatter myself," I rejoined mildly, "that the
two months' imprisonment that I have already undergone will seem to him a sufficient expiation?"

He promised to speak to him about it if I so desired. I begged him urgently to do me this good turn.
He informed me two days later that G . . . M . . .
had been so touched by the good things he had heard
about me that he not only appeared disposed to let
me out, but had even shown much desire to know
me better and proposed to pay me a visit in my
prison. Although his presence could be no pleasure
to me, I regarded it as a step in the direction of my
liberty.

Indeed he did come to Saint-Lazare. I found his
manner more grave and less foolish than it had been
in Manon's house. He made some sensible remarks
about my bad conduct. He added, apparently to justify

his own disorders, that human weakness was allowed to procure certain pleasures that nature demands, but that swindling and shameful tricks deserved to be punished. I listened to him with an air of submission with which he appeared satisfied. I did not even take offense at hearing him emit a few jokes about my brotherly relationship with Lescaut and Manon and about the little chapel,[36] of which, he told me, he supposed I must have done a great number at Saint-Lazare, since I found such pleasure in that pious occupation. But, unhappily for him and for myself, he let slip the remark that Manon too must have done some very pretty ones at the Hôpital.[37] In spite of the shudder that the name Hôpital caused me, I still had enough control to ask him mildly to explain himself.

"Oh yes," he replied, "for the last two months she has been learning good behavior at the Hôpital Général, and I hope she has profited from it as much as you have at Saint-Lazare."

If eternal imprisonment or death itself had been staring me in the face, I could not have mastered my fury at this frightful news. I hurled myself upon him in such a frenzy of rage that it used up half my strength. I had enough, nevertheless, to throw him on his back to the floor and take him by the throat. I was strangling him, when the noise of his fall and a few sharp cries, which I barely left him free to utter, brought the Superior and several monks into my room. They delivered him out of my hands. I myself had almost lost my strength and my breath.

"O God!" I cried, with a thousand sighs. "Heavenly justice! Must I live another moment after such infamy?"

I tried to throw myself again upon the barbarian who had just destroyed me. They stopped me. My despair, my cries, and my tears were beyond imagining. My behavior was so astounding that all the onlookers, who did not know the cause, stared at one

36 See note (31), p. 79.
37 See note (6), p. 23.

another with as much alarm as surprise. Meanwhile Monsieur de G . . . M . . . was readjusting his wig and his cravat; and, in his resentment at having been so roughly handled, he was ordering the Superior to lock me up tighter than ever and chastise me with all the punishments that are known to be appropriate at Saint-Lazare.

"No, sir," said the Superior, "it is not with a person of the Chevalier's birth that we deal in that way. Moreover, he is so gentle and honorable that it is hard for me to understand his having gone to this extreme without strong reasons."

This reply left Monsieur de G . . . M . . . completely disconcerted. He departed, saying that he would be able to make us bow down, the Superior and me and anyone who dared resist him.

The Superior, having ordered his monks to show him out, remained alone with me. He conjured me to tell him promptly the cause of this outburst.

"Oh, Father," I said to him, continuing to cry like a child, "picture the most horrible cruelty, imagine the most detestable of all barbarities: that is the action that the unworthy G . . . M . . . has been coward enough to commit. Oh! He has pierced my heart. I shall never get over it. I want to tell you the whole story," I added, sobbing. "You are good, you will have pity on me."

I gave him an abridged account of the long and insurmountable passion I had for Manon, the flourishing state of our fortune before we were robbed by our own servants, the offers that G . . . M . . . had made to my mistress, the bargain they had concluded, and the way it had been broken. True, I represented things to him in the most favorable light for us.

"That is the source," I went on, "of Monsieur de G . . . M . . . 's zeal for my conversion. He had the influence to have me locked up here for a motive of pure vengeance. I pardon him that; but, Father, that is not all: he had the dearest half of my very

self cruelly carried off, he had her shamefully put in
the Hôpital, he had the impudence to announce this
to me today with his own lips. In the Hôpital, Father! O Heaven! My charming mistress, my dear
queen in the Hôpital, like the most infamous of all
creatures! Where shall I find strength enough not to
die of grief and shame?"

The good Father, seeing me in this extreme afflic-
tion, undertook to console me. He told me that he
never had understood my adventure as I now related it; that he had indeed known that I was living
dissolutely, but he had supposed that what had
obliged Monsieur de G . . . M . . . to take an interest
was some relation, based on esteem and friendship,
with my family; that he had explained it to him only
on those terms; that what he had just learned from
me would bring a great change in my affairs, and
that he had no doubt that the faithful account he intended to give of this to the Lieutenant General of
Police could lead to my freedom.

He then asked me why I had not yet thought to
send news to my family, since they had had no part
in my captivity. I met this objection with a few
reasons drawn from the sorrow I had feared to cause
my father and the shame that I would have felt myself. Finally he promised to go at once to the Lieutenant General of Police, "if only," he added, "to
forestall some worse action by Monsieur de G . . .
M . . . , who left this house thoroughly dissatisfied,
and who is influential enough to make himself
feared."

I awaited the Father's return with all the agitation of a poor wretch just about to be sentenced.
For me it was an inexpressible torture to picture Manon at the Hôpital. Besides the infamy of the place,
I did not know in what manner she was being treated; and the memory of certain particulars that I
had heard concerning that house of horror renewed
my frenzy every moment. I was so determined to rescue her, at whatever cost and by whatever means, that

I would have set fire to Saint-Lazare if it had been impossible for me to get out any other way. So I thought
about the courses there were for me to take if it turned
out that the Lieutenant General of Police continued to
detain me there in spite of me. I put my ingenuity to
every test; I went over all the possibilities. I saw nothing
that could assure me of a certain escape, and I feared to
be locked up tighter if I made an unsuccessful attempt.
I remembered the names of a few friends from whom I
might hope for aid; but how could I let them know
my situation? At last I thought I had formed a plan
so adroit that it might work, and I put off arrang-
ing it still better until after the Father Superior's return, in case his action proved useless and made it
necessary.

He was not long in coming back. I did not see
on his face the signs of joy that accompany good
news.

"I spoke to the Lieutenant General of Police," he
told me, "but I spoke to him too late. Monsieur de
G . . . M . . . went to see him on leaving here, and
so prejudiced him against you that he was on the
point of sending me new orders to lock you up tighter. However, when I told him the whole story of
your affairs, he seemed to grow much milder; and,
laughing a bit at old Monsieur de G . . . M . . .'s in-
continence, he told me he would have to leave you
here six months to satisfy him—all the better for
you, he said, since your stay could not fail to be useful to you. He urged me to treat you honorably, and
I warrant you will have no cause to complain of
my ways."

This explanation by the good Superior was long
enough to give me time to make one prudent reflection. I recognized that I would risk upsetting my
plans if I showed him too much eagerness for my
freedom. I indicated to him, on the contrary, that
since it was necessary for me to remain, it was a
sweet consolation for me to have some share in his
esteem. I then asked him, unaffectedly, to grant me

one favor, which was of no importance to anyone
and which would do much for my peace of mind;
this was to notify one of my friends, a holy church-
man who lived at Saint-Sulpice, that I was in Saint-
Lazare, and to allow me to receive a visit from him
sometimes. This favor was granted me without hesitation.

The man in question was my friend Tiberge; not
that I hoped to get from him the help necessary for
my freedom; but I wanted to use him indirectly for
that purpose without his even knowing it. In a word,
here was my plan: I wanted to write to Lescaut and
charge him and our mutual friends with the task of
delivering me. The first difficulty was to get my letter into his hands; this was to be the function of
Tiberge. However, since Tiberge knew him to be my
mistress' brother, I feared he would have scruples
about undertaking this errand. My plan was to en-
close my letter to Lescaut in another letter which I
would address to a respectable acquaintance of
mine, asking him to deliver the first one promptly to
its address; and since it was necessary that I see Lescaut so that we could agree on our measures, I
wanted to instruct him to come to Saint-Lazare and
ask to see me under the name of my elder brother,
who supposedly had come to Paris expressly to take
cognizance of my affairs. I left to be considered with
him the means that should seem to us the most ex-
peditious and the surest.

The Father Superior had Tiberge notified of my
desire to see him. That faithful friend had not so wholly
lost sight of me as not to know all about my adventure;
he knew that I was at Saint-Lazare, and possibly he had
not been sorry about this disgrace, which he thought
might bring me back to the path of duty. He immediately hastened to my room.

Our conversation was most friendly. He wanted to
be informed about my intentions. I opened my heart
to him without reservation, except about my plan for
escape.

"It is not in your eyes, dear friend," I said to him, "that I have any wish to appear to be what I am not. If you thought to find here a friend sober and temperate in his desires, a libertine awakened by the chastisements of Heaven, in a word a heart freed of love and recovered from the charms of his Manon, you have judged me too favorably. You see me again just as you left me four months ago: ever tender, and ever unhappy by that fatal tenderness in which I never tire of seeking my happiness."

He replied that this admission made me inexcusable; that there were many sinners so intoxicated with the false happiness of vice as to prefer it openly to that of virtue; but that they were at least clinging to images of happiness, and that they were duped by appearances; but that to recognize as I did that the object of my attachment was fit only to make me guilty and unhappy, and to continue voluntarily to plunge myself into misfortune and crime, was a contradiction between ideas and conduct that did no honor to my reason.

"Tiberge," I retorted, "how easy it is for you to conquer when your weapons are unopposed! Let me reason a bit in turn. Can you claim that what you call the happiness of virtue is free from pains, disappointments, and anxieties? What name will you give to prison, the cross, the executions and tortures of tyrants? Will you say, as the mystics do, that what torments the body is happiness to the soul? You would not dare say so; it is an indefensible paradox. So this happiness that you exalt so highly is mingled with a thousand sufferings, or, to speak more accurately, is nothing but a web of unhappinesses through which one strives toward felicity. Now if the power of the imagination makes men find pleasure in these very ills, because they may lead to a happy goal for which we hope, why do you label as contradictory and senseless, in my conduct, a completely similar disposition? I love Manon; I strive through a thousand pains to live happy and tranquil with her.

The road I tread is unhappy, but the hope of arriving at my goal always spreads a certain sweetness over it; and I shall think myself only too well repaid, by one moment spent with her, for all the troubles I suffer to obtain it. So all things appear to me equal on your side and mine; or if there is some difference, it is still to my advantage, for the happiness I hope for is near, and the other is far off; mine is of the same nature as the pains, that is to say perceptible to the body; and the other is of a nature unknown, which is certain only through faith."

Tiberge appeared horrified by this reasoning. He took two steps backward, saying to me in the most serious way that what I had just said was not only an offense to good sense but also a wretched sophism born of impiety and irreligion. "For this comparison," he added, "between the goal of your sufferings and that which is proposed by religion is a most libertine and monstrous idea."

"I admit," I replied, "that it is not a just one; but take good note, it is not on this that my reasoning bears. My intent was to explain what you regard as a contradiction, in my perseverance in an unhappy love, and I think I have very well proven that if it is one, you cannot escape it any more than I. It was in that respect alone that I treated the matters as equal, and I still maintain that they are. Will you answer that the goal of virtue is infinitely superior to that of love? Who disputes that? But is that the point in question? Isn't the issue the power they both have to make us endure suffering? Let us judge by the effects. How many deserters we find from strict virtue, and how few you will find from love! Will you still answer that if there are sufferings in the practice of goodness they are not infallible and necessary; that tyrants and crosses are no longer to be found, and that great numbers of virtuous people are seen to lead a sweet and tranquil life? I will say likewise that there are peaceful and fortunate loves; and I will add what makes still another difference which is strongly to my advantage: that love, although it is rather often deceitful, at least promises only satisfactions and joys, whereas religion wants us to expect a sad and mortifying observance."

"Don't be alarmed," I added, seeing his zeal ready to fret. "The only conclusion I want to reach here is that there is no worse way to turn a heart away from love than to decry its delights and promise more happiness in the exercise of virtue. From the way we are made, it is certain that our felicity consists in pleasure: I defy anyone to form another idea of it; now the heart has no need for long consultation with itself to feel that of all pleasures the sweetest are those of love. It soon perceives that it is being deceived when it is promised more delightful ones elsewhere; and this deceit disposes it to mistrust the most solid of promises. Preachers who want to lead me back to virtue tell me that it is indispensably necessary, but do not disguise the fact that it is severe and painful. Establish the fact that the delights of love are fleeting, that they are forbidden, that they will be followed by eternal sufferings, and, what will perhaps make an even greater impression on me, that the more they are sweet and charming the more magnificently will Heaven reward so great a sacrifice; but confess that with hearts such as we have, they are our most perfect felicities here below."

This conclusion to my speech restored his good humor to Tiberge. He agreed that there was some reason in my thoughts. The only objection he added was to ask why I did not at least follow out my own principles by sacrificing my love to the hope of that remuneration of which I had so great an idea.

"Oh, my dear friend!" I replied. "Here is where I recognize my misery and my weakness. Alas! Yes, it is my duty to act according as I reason! But is action within my power? What aid would I not need in order to forget Manon's charms?"

"God forgive me," answered Tiberge, "I think we have another of our Jansenists[38] here."

"I don't know what I am," I replied, "and I don't see too clearly what one ought to be; but I feel only too strongly the truth of what they say."

This conversation served at least to renew my friend's pity. He understood that there was more weakness than wickedness in my disorders. His friendship was all the more disposed, later on, to give me help without which I should infallibly have perished of misery. However, I did not give him the slightest hint of the plan I had to escape from Saint-Lazare. I merely asked him to take charge of my letter. I had prepared it before he came, and I had no lack of pretexts to lend color to my need of writing. A faithful friend, he delivered it as requested, and before the day was over Lescaut received the one that was for him.

He came to see me the next day and passed himself off successfully under the name of my brother. I was overjoyed at seeing him in my room. I closed the door carefully.

"Let's not lose a single moment," I said to him. "First tell me the news of Manon, and then give me some good advice for breaking my chains."

He assured me that he had not seen his sister since the day before her imprisonment; that he had learned her fate and mine only by dint of inquiries and efforts; that when he had presented himself two or three times at the Hôpital, he had been refused permission to talk to her.

"Miserable G . . . M . . . ," I exclaimed, "you shall pay me dear for this!"

"As regards your liberation," Lescaut went on, "that is not as easy an undertaking as you think. We spent the evening yesterday, two of my friends and

[38] A rigorous Catholic sect, opposed to the Jesuits, strong in France from the mid-seventeeth to the mid-eighteenth century, though condemned by Pope Clement XI in 1713. The point of Tiberge's remark is their belief in predestination.

I, observing all the outside of this place, and we judged that since your windows are on a court surrounded by buildings, as you had mentioned to us, it would be very difficult to get you out of there. Moreover, you are on the fourth floor, and we cannot bring in either ropes or ladders. So I see no resource from the outside. It is in the building itself that we must think of some scheme."

"No," I retorted, "I have examined everything, especially since my confinement has been a little less rigorous, thanks to the Superior's kindness. The door to my room is no longer locked. I am free to walk about in the monks' galleries; but all the stairways are blocked by thick doors which they are careful to keep closed night and day; so that it is impossible that dexterity alone can rescue me. Wait," I added, after thinking a bit about an idea that seemed excellent to me; "could you bring me a pistol?"

"Easily," said Lescaut; "but do you want to kill someone?"

I assured him that I had so little intention of killing that the pistol did not even need to be loaded.

"Bring it to me tomorrow," I added, "and don't fail to be opposite the door to this place at eleven o'clock in the evening with two or three of our friends. I hope I shall be able to join you there."

He urged me in vain to tell him more about it. I said that an enterprise such as I was contemplating could not seem reasonable until after it had succeeded. I asked him to cut his visit short so that he would have an easier time seeing me the next day. He was admitted with as little trouble as the first time. His manner was grave. There is no one who would not have taken him for a man of honor.

When I found myself equipped with the instrument of my liberation, I had almost no further doubt of the success of my plan. It was bizarre and daring; but what was I not capable of, with the motives that animated me? From the time that I had been allowed to leave my room and walk about in the gal-

leries, I had noticed that the porter brought the
keys of all the doors to the Superior every evening,
and that after this a deep silence reigned throughout
the house, showing that everyone had gone to bed.
By a communicating gallery I could go without any
obstacle from my room to the Father's. My resolution was to take his keys from him, frightening him
with my pistol if he made any difficulty about giving
them to me, and to use them to gain the street. I
waited impatiently for the moment. The porter came
at the ordinary time, that is to say a little after
nine. I let one more hour pass, to be sure that all
the monks and servants were alseep. Finally I set
out, with my weapon and a lighted candle. I first
knocked softly on the Father's door, to awaken him
without noise. He heard me at the second knock;
and, no doubt imagining that it was one of the monks
who was feeling sick and needed help, he got up to
open the door for me. He took the precaution, however, of asking, through the door, who it was and
what was wanted. I was obliged to give my name,
but I affected a plaintive tone to give him to understand that I was not feeling well.

"Ah, it is you, my dear son," he said to me, opening the door. "Now what is it that brings you here
so late?"

I went into his room, and having drawn him to
the other end away from the door, I declared to him
that it was impossible for me to stay at Saint-Lazare
any longer; that night was a convenient time for leaving unperceived, and that I was relying on him, as a
friend, to consent to open the doors for me or to
lend me his keys to open them with myself.

This compliment was bound to surprise him. He
remained for some time looking at me without answering. Since I had no time to lose, I spoke up again
and told him that I was very touched by all his
kindnesses, but that since freedom was the most precious of all goods, especially for me from whom it
was being unjustly snatched away, I was resolved to

procure it that very night, whatever the price; and for fear he might have an impulse to raise his voice and call for help, I showed him a worthy reason for silence, which I was holding under my jacket.

"A pistol!" he said. "What! My son, do you want to take my life, in return for the consideration I have shown you?"

"God forbid," I answered. "You have too much sense and reason to put me to that necessity; but I want to be free, and I am so resolved on it that if my plan fails through your fault, it's all up with you."

"But my dear son," he replied, looking pale and frightened, "what have I done to you? What reason do you have to want my death?"

"No, no!" I returned impatiently. "I have no intention of killing you if you want to live. Open the door for me and I am your best friend."

I noticed the keys, which were on the table. I took them and asked him to follow me, making as little noise as he could. He was obliged to make up his mind to it. As we moved along and he opened another door, he kept repeating with a sigh:

"Ah, my son, ah! Who would ever have believed it?"

"No noise, Father," I repeated in turn at every moment.

At last we reached a sort of barrier that stands in front of the big door to the street. I thought myself already free, and I was behind the Father, with my candle in one hand and my pistol in the other. While he was busy opening it, a servant, who slept in a little adjoining room, hearing the noise of some of the bolts, gets up and puts his head out of his door. The good Father apparently thought him capable of stopping me. He ordered him very imprudently to come to his rescue. He was a powerful rascal, and hurled himself upon me without hesitating. I had no pity for him; I fired my shot right through the middle of his chest.

"See what you have caused, Father," I said rather

spiritedly to my guide. "But don't let that keep you from finishing," I added, pushing him toward the last door.

He dared not refuse to open it. I went out without mishap, and a few paces away I found Lescaut, who was waiting for me with two friends, as he had promised. We went off. Lescaut asked me if he had not heard a pistol fired.

"That's your fault," I told him; "why did you bring it to me loaded?"

However, I thanked him for having taken that precaution, without which I would no doubt have been at Saint-Lazare for a long time. We went and spent the night at a tavern, where I made up a bit for the bad cheer I had made for nearly three months. I could not, however, give myself up to pleasure. I suffered mortally for Manon.

"We must deliver her," I said to my three friends. "I have wished for liberty only with that in view. I ask you for the aid of your skill; as for me, I shall stake my very life."

Lescaut, who did not lack wit and prudence, pointed out that we must go bridle in hand; that my escape from Saint-Lazare, and the mishap that had occurred as I left, would infallibly cause a stir; that the Lieutenant General of Police would institute a search for me, and his arms were long; in short, that if I did not want to be exposed to something worse than Saint-Lazare, I would do well to stay under cover and indoors for a few days, to give the first fire of my enemies' anger time to go out. His advice was wise; but I would have had to be equally so to follow it. So much slowness and circumspection did not accord with my passion. The most I would consent to was to promise him that I would spend the next day sleeping. He locked me in my room, where I remained until evening.

I employed part of this time in fashioning plans and expedients for rescuing Manon. I was fully convinced that her prison was even more impenetrable than mine had been. Force and violence were out of the question, artifice was needed; but the goddess of invention herself would not have known where to begin. I could see so little daylight that I put off a better consideration of things until I should have gained some information about the internal arrangements of the Hôpital.

As soon as night had restored my liberty, I asked Lescaut to accompany me. We struck up a conversation with one of the porters, who seemed to us a man of good sense. I pretended to be a stranger in town who had heard wonderful things about the Hôpital Général and the order observed in it. I questioned him about the most minute details; and from one item to another we came to the administrators, whose names and quality I begged him to tell me. The answers he made on this last point gave me an idea on which I immediately congratulated myself and which I lost no time in putting into effect. I asked him (as a thing essential to my plan) whether these gentlemen had any children. He told me that he could not give me an exact account, but that as for Monsieur de T..., who was one of the most important, he knew that he had a son old enough to be married, who had come to the Hôpital several times with his father. This was enough assurance for me. I broke off our conversation almost immediately and confided to Lescaut, on the way back to his house, the plan I had formed.

"I imagine," I told him, "that young Monsieur de T..., who is rich and of good family, has a certain taste for pleasures, like most young men of his age. He cannot be a woman-hater, nor so ridiculous as to refuse his services in a matter of love. The plan I have formed is to interest him in Manon's freedom. If he is a man of honor and feeling, he will grant us his help out of generosity. If he is not capable of being led by that motive, at least he will do something for a charming girl, if only in the hope of having a share in her favors. I do not want to put off seeing him," I added, "beyond tomorrow. I feel so consoled by this plan that I take it as a good omen."

Lescaut himself agreed that there was plausibility in my ideas and that we might hope for something by this course. I spent the night less sadly for it.

Morning having come, I dressed as nicely as I could in my present state of indigence and took a cab to Monsieur de T . . . 's house. He was surprised to receive a visit from an unknown. I augured well from his face and his courtesy. I explained myself to him naturally; and to arouse his natural feelings, I spoke to him of my passion and my mistress' merit as of two things that could be equaled only by each other. He told me that although he had never seen Manon, he had heard of her, at least if she was the one who had been the mistress of old G . . . M . . . . I had no doubt that he was informed of the part I had played in that adventure; and to win him more and more by giving myself merit for my frankness, I told him the details of all that had happened to Manon and me.

"You see, sir," I went on, "that the welfare of my life and that of my heart are now in your hands. The one is no dearer to me than the other. I have no reserve with you, because I am informed of your generosity, and because the similarity in our ages makes me hope there will be some in our inclinations."

He seemed very sensible to this sign of openness and candor. His reply was that of a man of the world and a man of feelings—which the world does not always give, and often makes us lose. He told me that he placed my visit among his strokes of good fortune, that he would regard my friendship as one of his happiest acquisitions, and that he would strive to deserve it by the ardor of his services. He did not promise to restore Manon to me, because, he said, he had only a moderate and uncertain influence; but he offered to procure me the pleasure of seeing her and to do everything in his power to return her to my arms. I was more satisfied with this uncertainty about his influence than I would have been with a complete assurance of fulfilling all my desires. I found, in the moderation of his offers, a sign of frankness which charmed me. In a word, I promised myself all success from his good offices. The promise to have me see Manon would alone have made me undertake anything whatever for him. I indicated to him something of these feelings, in a way that convinced him too that I was not ill born. We embraced each other tenderly and became friends for no other reason than the goodness of our hearts and a simple inclination that leads one tender and generous man to love another who is like him.

He carried the proofs of his esteem much further; for having put my adventures together in his mind, and judging that on getting out of Saint-Lazare I must not be well off, he offered me his purse and urged me to accept it. I did not accept it; but I said to him:

"This is too much, my dear sir. If with all this kindness and friendliness you let me see my dear Manon again, I am yours for life. If you restore that dear creature to me for good, I shall not think myself quit if I shed all my blood in serving you."

We parted only after agreeing on the time and place where we should meet again. He was complaisant enough not to put me off beyond the afternoon of the same day. I waited for him in a coffeehouse, where he came to join me around four o'clock, and we set out together for the Hôpital. My knees were trembling as I crossed the courtyard.

"O power of love!" said I. "So once again I shall see the idol of my heart, the object of so many tears and anxieties! Heaven! Keep me alive long enough to go to her, and after that dispose as you will of my fortune and my days; I have no other favor to ask of you."

Monsieur de T . . . spoke to various warders of the

place, who eagerly offered him everything that depended on them for his satisfaction. He had himself
shown the section where Manon had her room, and
we were taken there along with a key of frightening size which served to open her door. I asked the
servant who was guiding us, and who was the one
responsible for looking after her, how she had spent
her time in this abode. He told us that hers was an
angelic sweetness; that he had never had a harsh
word from her; that she had continually shed tears
for the first six weeks after her arrival, but that for
some time now she had seemed to take her misfortune with more patience and was busy sewing from
morning to evening, except for a few hours that she
spent reading. I asked him further whether she had
been properly provided for. He assured me that she
had at least never lacked the necessities.

We approached the door. My heart was beating
violently. I said to Monsieur de T . . . :

"Go in alone and prepare her for my visit, for I
fear she may be too overcome if she sees me all of
a sudden."

The door was opened for us. I remained in the
corridor. Nevertheless I heard what they said. He
told her that he had come to bring her a little consolation; that he was a friend of mine, and that he
took much interest in our happiness. She asked him
with the greatest eagerness if she might learn from
him what had become of me. He promised to bring
me to her feet, as tender, as faithful as she could
wish.

"When?" she asked.

"This very day," he said to her; "this blessed moment will not be long in coming; he will appear this
instant if you like."

She understood that I was at the door. I entered
as she was rushing headlong toward it. We embraced
with that effusive tenderness that three months' absence renders so charming to perfect lovers. Our
sighs, our interrupted exclamations, a thousand lov-

ers' names repeated languorously by each one,
formed, for a quarter of an hour, a scene that
touched Monsieur de T . . . .

"I envy you," he said to me as he had us
sit down; "there is no glorious lot to which I would
not prefer so beautiful and so passionate a mistress."

"Even so would I disdain all the empires in the
world," I replied "to assure myself of the happiness
of being loved by her."

All the rest of a conversation so ardently desired
could not fail to be infinitely tender. Poor Manon told me her adventures and I related mine. We
wept bitterly as we talked of the condition she was
in and the one from which I had only just escaped.
Monsieur de T . . . consoled us by fresh promises to
strive ardently to end our miseries. He advised us
not to make this first interview too long, so as to
make it easier for him to procure us others. He had
great difficulty in giving us any relish for this advice; Manon especially could not bring herself to let
me go. A hundred times she pulled me back onto
my chair. She held me back by my clothes and by
my hands.

"Alas! In what a place you are leaving me!" she
kept saying. "Who can assure me that I will see you
again?"

Monsieur de T . . . promised to come and see her
often with me.

"As for the place," he added pleasantly, "we must
call it the Hôpital no longer; it is Versailles, since a
person who deserves to rule over all hearts is here
confined."

On the way out I gave some money to the valet
who served her, to engage him to be zealous in his
care. This man had a soul less base and hard than
his fellows. He had been a witness of our interview;
this tender spectacle had touched him. A louis d'or,
which I presented to him, finished winning him over
to me. He took me aside as we went down into the
courtyards.

"Sir," he said to me, "if you want to take me into your service, or give me a proper reward to compensate me for the loss of the job I hold here, I think it will be easy for me to liberate Mademoiselle Manon."

I opened my ear to this proposal; and although I was in almost complete privation, I made him promises far above his desires. I reckoned confidently that it would always be easy to recompense a man of his stamp.

"Rest assured, my friend," I said to him, "that there is nothing I will not do for you, and that your future is as assured as mine."

I asked to know what means he intended to employ.

"None other," said he, "than to open the door of her room for her one evening, and take her to you as far as the street door, where you will have to be ready to receive her."

I asked him whether it was not to be feared that she would be recognized as she went through the corridors and the courtyards. He confessed that there was some danger, but said that some risk had to be taken. Although I was delighted to see him so resolute, I called Monsieur de T . . . to tell him about this plan and the only reason that seemed possibly to make it doubtful. He saw more difficulty in it than I. He agreed that she might possibly escape in this manner.

"But," he went on, "if she is recognized, if she is arrested while fleeing, it may be all up with her forever. Besides, you would have to leave Paris instantly, for you would never be well enough hidden from search. This would be redoubled, as much on your account as hers. A man escapes easily enough when he is alone; but it is almost impossible to remain unknown with a pretty woman."

Solid as this reasoning appeared to me, it could not win out in my mind over so immediate a hope of setting Manon free. I said so to Monsieur de T . . . , and I begged him to forgive a little imprudence and rashness in love. I added that my intention was indeed to leave Paris and stay, as I had already done, in some neighboring village. We therefore agreed with the valet not to put off his undertaking beyond the next day, and, to make it as sure as it was in our power to do, we resolved to bring men's clothes with a view to facilitating our exit. It was not easy to get them in, but my ingenuity did not fail me for finding a way. I merely asked Monsieur de T . . . to put on two light waistcoats the next day, one on top of the other, and I took charge of all the rest.

In the morning we went back to the Hôpital. I had with me, for Manon, linen, stockings, and so on, and over my jacket an overcoat that revealed nothing too bulging about my pockets. We were only a moment in her room. Monsieur de T . . . left her one of his two waistcoats; I gave her my jacket, since my overcoat was enough for me to go out in. Nothing was lacking for her costume except the breeches, which unluckily I had forgotten. My forgetting this necessary item would no doubt have made us laugh if the predicament it placed us in had been less serious. I was in despair that a trifle of this nature was capable of stopping us. However, I made my decision, which was to go out myself without breeches. I left mine to Manon. My overcoat was long, and with the aid of a few pins I put myself in shape to get decently past the door.

The rest of the day seemed to me unbearably long. Finally, night having come, we went in a carriage up near the door of the Hôpital. We were not there long before we saw Manon appear with her escort. Our door was open, and in a moment they both climbed in. I clasped my dear mistress in my arms. She was trembling like a leaf. The coachman asked me where he was to drive to.

"Drive to the end of the world," I told him, "take me some place where I can never be parted from Manon."

This outburst, which I could not master, nearly

brought me serious trouble. The coachman reflected
on my words, and when I later told him the name
of the street to which we wanted to be driven, he
answered that he was afraid I was involving him in
some bad business; that he could see very well that
this handsome young man named Manon was a girl
I was carrying off from the Hôpital, and that he was
of no mind to ruin himself for love of me. This rascal's delicacy was nothing but the wish to make me
pay more for the carriage. We were too near the
Hôpital not to put up with it.

"Hold your tongue," I told him, "there's a louis
d'or to earn for you."

After that he would have helped me burn down
the Hôpital itself. We reached the house where Lescaut was living. Since it was late, Monsieur de T . . .
left us on the way, promising to see us again the
next day. The valet alone remained with us.

I was holding Manon clasped so tightly in my
arms that we occupied only one seat in the coach.
She was weeping for joy, and I felt her tears wetting
my face. But when it was time to get out and
enter Lescaut's house, I had another altercation with
the coachman, which had disastrous consequences. I
repented of having promised him a louis, not only because the gift was excessive, but also for a much
stronger reason, which was my inability to pay it. I
sent for Lescaut. He came down from his room and
to the door. I whispered in his ear the embarrassment I was in. Since he was quick of temper and
not in the habit of humoring a coachman, he told
me I was joking.

"A louis d'or!" he added. "Twenty blows with a
cane for that rascal!"

In vain did I point out to him gently that he was
going to ruin us; he snatched my cane from me as
though to beat the coachman with it. The latter,
who may at some time have had the misfortune to
feel the hand of a guardsman or a musketeer, fled
in fright with his carriage, shouting that I had cheat-

ed him but that I would hear from him. Again and again I told him to stop, but in vain. His flight caused me extreme anxiety. I had no doubt that he would notify the police.

"You've ruined me," I said to Lescaut; "I would not be safe at your house; we must get away this moment."

I gave Manon my arm, and we promptly left that dangerous street on foot. Lescaut kept us company.

It is a marvelous thing how Providence links up events. Hardly had we been walking for five or six minutes when a man whose face I could not discern recognized Lescaut. No doubt he was looking for him in the neighborhood of his house, with the fell plan which he now carried out.

"It's Lescaut," he said, firing a pistol at him; "he will go sup with the angels tonight."

He ran away immediately. Lescaut fell without the slightest sign of life. I urged Manon to flee, for our help was useless to a corpse, and I feared to be arrested by the watch, which could not fail to appear soon. With her and the valet I turned into the first little cross street. She was so frantic that I had trouble supporting her. At last I spied a cab at the end of the street. We climbed in. But when the coachman asked me where to take us, I was at a loss to answer him. I had no safe refuge, no trusty friend to whom I dared have recourse. I was out of money, having hardly more than half a pistole in my purse. Fright and fatigue had so overcome Manon that she was half swooning beside me. Moreover my imagination was full of the murder of Lescaut, and I was not yet free of apprehension about the watch. What was I to do? I fortunately remembered the inn at Chaillot, where I had spent a few days with Manon when we had gone to live in that village. I hoped not only to be in safety there, but to be able to live for some time without being pressed to pay.

"Take us to Chaillot," I said to the coachman.

He refused to go there so late unless for a pistole:

further embarrassment. Finally we agreed on six francs: that was all there was left in my purse.

I was consoling Manon as we went along; but inwardly there was despair in my heart. I would have killed myself a thousand times if I had not had in my arms the only good that attached me to life. This thought alone restored me.

"At least I have her," I said to myself; "she loves me, she is mine: Tiberge may say what he likes, this is no phantom of happiness. I could see the whole universe perish and take no interest. Why? Because I have no affection left over."

This feeling was genuine; however, at the very time I was setting so little store by the goods of the world, I felt that I would have needed to have at least a little share of them to attain an even more sovereign disdain for all the rest. Love is stronger than plenty, stronger than treasures and riches, but it needs their help; and nothing makes a delicate lover more desperate than to see himself dragged down by that, in spite of himself, to the coarseness of the basest souls.

It was eleven o'clock when we arrived in Chaillot. We were received at the inn as old acquaintances. No one was surprised to see Manon in man's clothing because people are accustomed, in Paris and the environs, to see women assume all sorts of disguises. I had her served as nicely as if I had been in the best of fortunes. She did not know I was low in money. I was very careful not to tell her anything about it, being resolved to go back to Paris alone the next day and seek some remedy for this vexatious sort of malady.

At supper she seemed to me pale and thinner. I had not noticed it at the Hôpital because the room in which I had seen her was not of the best-lit. I asked her if this was not another effect of the fright she had had in seeing her brother murdered. She assured me that however upset she was by that accident, her

pallor came only from having suffered my absence for
three months.

"So you do love me terribly?" I asked.

"A thousand times more than I can say," she replied.

"Then you will never leave me again?" I added.

"No, never," she answered, and that assurance was
confirmed by so many caresses and vows that it
seemed to me indeed impossible that she could ever
forget them.

I have always been convinced that she was sincere;
what reason would she have had to dissemble to such
a point? But she was even more fickle yet; or rather
she was not anything any more, and she did not even
recognize herself, when, having before her eyes wom-
en living in abundance, she found herself in poverty
and need. I was on the eve of having a final proof
of this, which surpassed all the others and brought
about the strangest adventure that has ever happened
to a man of my birth and my fortune.

Since I knew this to be her temperament, I made
haste the next day to go to Paris. Her brother's
death, and the need to have linen and clothes for
her and for me, were such good reasons that no pretexts were necessary. I left the inn with the intention, so I told Manon and my host, of taking a hired
carriage; but that was bravado. Since necessity obliged
me to go on foot, I walked very fast as far as the
Cours-la-Reine, where I planned to stop. I had to
have a moment of solitude and tranquillity to com-
pose myself and plan what I was going to do in Paris.

I sat down on the grass. I plunged into a sea of
reasonings and reflections, which little by little came
down to three principal points.

I needed some immediate help for an infinite
number of personal necessities. I had to seek some
course that would at least open up to me hopes for
the future; and, no less important, I had to get information and take measures for Manon's security and
mine. After exhausting myself in plans and combina-

tions under these three headings, I further judged it best to cut out the last two. We were not in bad cover in a Chaillot room; and as for future needs, I decided it would be time to think of them when I had satisfied our present ones.

So the question was how to fill my purse right now. Monsieur de T . . . had generously offered me his; but I felt an extreme repugnance at reminding him myself of this matter. What a part to play, to go and expose one's misery to a stranger and ask him to share his wealth with us! It is only a base soul that could be capable of it, by a meanness that keeps him from feeling the indignity; or a humble Christian, by an excess of nobility that makes him superior to this shame. I was neither a base man nor a good Christian; I would have given half my blood to avoid this humiliation.

"Tiberge," I said to myself, "kind Tiberge, will he refuse me what he has the power to give me? No, he will be touched by my misery; but he will murder me with his moralizing. I will have to endure his reproaches, his exhortations, his threats; he will make me buy his help so dear that I would give still another part of my blood rather than expose myself to this trying scene, which will leave me disturbed and remorseful. All right!" I went on. "Then I must give up all hope, since I have no other course left and I am so far from determining on those two that I would rather shed half my blood than take one, that is to say all my blood rather than take both.—Yes, all my blood," I added after a moment's reflection; "I would rather give it, no doubt, than bring myself to base supplications. But my blood, is that at issue here? At issue is Manon's life and support; at issue is her love and her fidelity. What is there that I would put in the scales against her? I have never put anything there up to now. She takes the place for me of glory, happiness, and fortune. There are many things, no doubt, that I would give my life to obtain or avoid; but to prize a thing more than my life is not a reason for prizing it as much as I do Manon."

I was not long in reaching my decision, after this reasoning. I continued on my way, resolved to go first to Tiberge, and from there to Monsieur de T . . . .

On entering Paris I took a cab, although I had nothing to pay for it with; I was counting on the help that I was going to solicit. I had myself driven to the Luxembourg, where I sent word to Tiberge that I was waiting for him. He satisfied my impatience by his promptness. I told him the extremity of my needs, with no equivocation. He asked me whether the hundred pistoles that I had returned to him would be enough; and, without offering any difficulty by so much as a word, he went and got them for me that instant, with that open manner and that pleasure in giving that is known only to love and true friendship.

Although I had not had the slightest doubt of the success of my request, I was surprised to have obtained it on such easy terms, that is to say without his scolding me for my impenitence. But I was wrong in thinking myself wholly quit of his reproaches; for when he had finished counting out his money to me and I was preparing to leave him, he asked me to take a walk along one of the paths with him. I had not spoken to him of Manon; he did not know that she was at liberty; thus his moralizing bore only on my rash flight from Saint-Lazare and the fear he had that instead of profiting by the lessons in wisdom I had received there I might resume the path of disorder. He told me that having gone to visit me at Saint-Lazare the day after my escape, he had been shocked beyond all expression on learning the way I had gotten out; he had had a talk with the Superior about it; the good Father was not yet recovered from his fright, nevertheless he had had the generosity to disguise the circumstances of my departure to the Lieutenant General of Police, and had kept the porter's death from being known outside; thus I had no cause for alarm on that score; but if I had the slightest sense of wisdom left, I would profit by this happy turn which Heaven had given to my affairs; I should begin by writing to my father and putting myself right with him; and if for once I was willing to follow his advice, it was his opinion that I should leave Paris and return to the bosom of my family.

I listened to his talk to the end. There were many satisfying things in it. I was delighted, in the first place, to have nothing to fear on account of Saint-Lazare. The streets of Paris became a free country for me again. In the second place, I congratulated myself that Tiberge had not the slightest idea of Manon's deliverance and her return to me. I even noticed that he had avoided speaking to me about her, apparently in the opinion that she had less hold on my heart, since I appeared so tranquil on that subject. I resolved, if not to return to my family, at least to write to my father, as he advised, and let him know that I was disposed to return to the path of duty and of his will. My hope was to induce him to send me some money on the pretext of taking up my training at the Academy; for I would have had trouble convincing him that I was of a mind to return to a career in the Church. And at bottom I had no aversion for what I meant to promise him. I was very pleased, on the contrary, to apply myself to something honorable and reasonable, as long as that plan could be reconciled with my love. I was counting on living with my mistress and at the same time receiving my training. That was thoroughly compatible. I was so satisfied with all these ideas that I promised Tiberge to send off a letter to my father that very day. And indeed, on leaving him, I went into a scrivener's and wrote in so tender and submissive a tone that on rereading my letter I flattered myself that I would obtain something from the paternal heart.

Although I was in a position to take and pay for a cab after leaving Tiberge, I made it my pleasure to go proudly on foot on my way to Monsieur de T . . . 's. I found joy in this exercise of my liberty, for which my friend had assured me there remained nothing to fear. However, it came to my mind all of a sudden that his assurances concerned only Saint-Lazare and that besides that I had the affair of the Hôpital on my hands, without counting the death of Lescaut, in which I was involved at least as a witness. This recollection frightened me so acutely that I drew back into the nearest alley and sent for a coach from there. I went straight to Monsieur de T . . . 's, who laughed at my fright. It seemed ridiculous even to me when he informed me that I had nothing to fear on either score, the Hôpital or Lescaut. He told me that with the thought that he might be suspected of having had a part in Manon's deliverance, he had gone to the Hôpital in the morning and asked to see her, pretending not to know what had happened; that they were so far from accusing either him or me that they had been eager, on the contrary, to tell him this adventure as a strange piece of news, and they marveled that a girl as pretty as Manon should have decided to escape with a servant; that he had contented himself with replying coldly that he was not surprised and that people will do anything for freedom.

He went on to tell me that from there he had gone to Lescaut's in the hope of finding me there with my charming mistress; that the landlord, who was a carriage maker, had protested that he had seen neither her nor me; but that it was no wonder that we had not appeared at his house, if it was to see Lescaut that we were to have come, because we would doubtless have learned that he had just been killed at about the same time. Whereupon he had not refused to explain what he knew about the cause and the circumstances of that death.

About two hours earlier a guardsman friend of Lescaut's had come to see him and proposed gambling. Lescaut had won so fast that the other had found himself a hundred crowns poorer in an hour, that is to say without any money. This wretch, who saw that he had not a sou, had begged Lescaut to lend him half the sum he had lost; and over some difficulties arising out of this occasion, they had quarreled with the utmost animosity. Lescaut had refused to go out with him and take to the sword, and the other, on leaving him, had sworn to blow his brains out; which he had done that very evening. Monsieur de T . . . was nice enough to add that he had been very worried about us and that he continued to offer me his services. I did not hesitate to tell him the place of our retreat. He asked me to approve his coming to supper with us.

Since all I had left to do was to get some linen and clothes for Manon, I told him that we could leave right then if he was willing to be kind enough to stop off for a moment with me at the stores of various merchants. I do not know whether he thought I made this proposition with a view to enlisting his generosity, or whether it was on the simple impulse of a fine soul; but, having consented to leave immediately, he took me to the merchants who supplied his own house; he had me choose several materials more expensive than I had planned on; and when I was preparing to pay them, he absolutely forbade the merchants to accept a sou from me. This gallant gesture was made so gracefully that I felt I could take advantage of it without shame. Together we took the road to Chaillot, where I arrived with less worry than I had left it.

The Chevalier des Grieux having spent more than an hour on this story, I begged him to take a little rest and keep us company for supper. Our attentiveness made him judge that we had listened to him with pleasure. He assured us that we should find something even more interesting in the sequel to his story; and when we had finished supper, he continued in these terms.

Story of Manon Lescaut

PART TWO

My presence and the civilities of Monsieur de T...
dispelled whatever chagrin might be left in Manon.

"Let's forget our past terrors, my dear heart," I
said to her when we arrived, "and let's begin to live
again happier than ever. After all, love is a good
master. Fortune could not possibly cause us as many
woes as love allows us to enjoy pleasures."

Our supper was a true scene of joy. I was proud-
er and happier with Manon and my hundred pistoles
than the richest tax collector in Paris with his piled-
up treasures. Riches must be reckoned by the means
we have to satisfy our desires. I had not a single one
unfulfilled. Even the future caused me little anxiety.
I was almost sure that my father would make no
trouble over giving me enough to live decently in
Paris, because, being in my twentieth year, I was
coming into my right to demand my share of my
mother's estate. I did not hide from Manon that the
total of my present funds was only one hundred
pistoles. That was enough to wait quietly for a better fortune, which it seemed could not fail me, either
by my natural rights or by the resources of gambling.

Thus[1] for the first few weeks I thought only of
enjoying my situation; and since my sense of honor,
as well as a lingering circumspection concerning the
police, made me put off from day to day rejoining

[1] The episode of the Italian prince, which begins here and
continues through "made me approve of everything" (p. 122)
is an addition of 1753.

the association of the Hôtel de T . . . ,[2] I confined myself to gambling in a few less discredited gatherings,
where fortune's favor spared me the humiliation of
having recourse to ingenuity. I used to go and spend
part of the afternoon in town and return for supper
to Chaillot, very often accompanied by Monsieur de
T . . . , whose friendship for us grew from day to day.
Manon found resources against boredom. She made
friends with a few young persons in the neighborhood
whom spring had brought back there. Walks and the
little occupations of their sex alternated in keeping
them busy. A bit of gambling, whose limits they had
prescribed, paid the cost of the carriage. They used
to go and take the air in the Bois de Boulogne; and
in the evening, on my return, I found Manon more
beautiful, happier, and more passionate than ever.

Nevertheless there arose a few clouds which seemed
to threaten the edifice of my happiness. But they
were clearly dispersed, and Manon's playful temper
made the upshot so comical that I still find sweetness
in a memory that brings back to me her tenderness and
the charms of her wit.

The single valet who composed our domestic staff
took me aside one day to tell me with much embarrassment that he had an important secret to
communicate to me. I encouraged him to speak freely.
After some circumlocution, he gave me to understand
that a foreign lord seemed to have conceived much love
for Mademoiselle Manon. The turmoil in my blood
could be felt in all my veins.

"Has she any for him?" I interrupted, more
brusquely than prudence allowed, in order to be enlightened.

My excitement frightened him. He answered me
with some uneasiness that his penetration had not
gone that far, but that having noticed for some days
that this foreigner came assiduously to the Bois de
Boulogne, got out of his carriage, and, setting out

[2] Transylvanie.

alone in the bypaths, seemed to be looking for a
chance to see or meet Mademoiselle, it had occurred
to him to strike up an acquaintance with his men, to
learn the name of their master; that they spoke of
him as an Italian prince and themselves suspected
him of some gallant adventure; that he had been unable to gain any further light on this (he added,
trembling) because the prince, having then come out
of the wood, had approached him familiarly and
asked him his name; after which, as if he had
guessed that he was in our service, he had congratulated him on belonging to the most charming person
in the world.

I was waiting impatiently for the sequel to this
story. He ended it with timid excuses, which I at-
tributed only to my imprudent agitation. In vain I
urged him to go on without disguise. He protested
to me that he knew nothing more and that, since
what he had just told me had happened the day before, he had not seen the prince's men again. I reassured
him, not only with praises, but with a respectable
reward; and without showing him the slightest mistrust
of Manon, I recommended to him in a calmer tone that
he keep watch on all the foreigner's movements.

In truth, his fright left me cruel doubts. It could
have made him suppress part of the truth. However,
after a few reflections, I recovered from my alarms
to the point of regretting that I had shown this sign
of weakness. I could not make it a crime in Manon
to be loved. There was much to suggest that she was
unaware of her conquest; and what sort of a life was
I going to live if I was capable of opening the gates
of my heart so easily to jealousy? I went back to
Paris the next day without having formed any other
plan than to hasten the progress of my fortune by
playing for bigger stakes, so as to put myself in a
position to leave Chaillot on the first occasion for uneasiness. That evening I learned nothing to disturb
my rest. The foreigner had again appeared at the
Bois de Boulogne, and assuming, from what had

happened the day before, the right to approach my confidant again, he had spoken to him of his love, but in terms which did not imply any understanding with Manon. He had questioned him about a thousand details. Finally, he had tried to win him over by considerable promises; and bringing out a letter that he had ready, he had offered him—in vain—several louis d'or to give it to his mistress.

Two days passed with no other incident. The third was more stormy. On arriving from town rather late, I learned that Manon, during her walk, had left her companions for a moment, and that when the foreigner, who had been following her at a short distance, had approached her on the sign she had made him, she had given him a letter which he had received with transports of joy. He had had time to express them only by amorously kissing the writing, because she had immediately fled. But she had appeared extraordinarily gay for the rest of the day; and since she had come back home this humor had not left her. I shuddered, I have no doubt, at each word.

"Are you quite sure," I said sadly to my valet, "that your eyes have not deceived you?"

He called Heaven to witness his good faith. I do not know to what lengths the torments of my heart would have borne me if Manon, who had heard me come in, had not come to meet me with an air of impatience and with complaints about my slowness. She did not wait for my reply to smother me with caresses; and when she found herself alone with me she reproached me very sharply for the habit I was getting into of coming home so late. Since my silence left her free to go on, she told me that for the past three weeks I had not spent one whole day with her; that she could not endure such long absences; that she asked of me at least one day, at intervals; and that the next day she wanted to see me beside her from morning to evening.

"I'll be there, have no doubt," I replied in a rather brusque tone.

She paid little attention to my chagrin; and in the impulse of her joy, which indeed seemed to me singularly keen, she gave me a thousand amusing sketches of the way she had spent the day. "Strange girl!" I said to myself. "What am I to expect from this prelude?"

The incident of our first parting came back to my mind. However, I thought I saw, in the basis for her joy and her caresses, an air of truth that was in accord with the appearances.

It was not hard for me to ascribe my sadness, from which I could not defend myself during our supper, to a loss I lamented having suffered at gambling. I had considered it an extreme advantage that the idea of my not leaving Chaillot the next day had come from her. That was gaining time for my deliberations. My presence removed all sorts of fears for the next day, and if I did not notice anything that obliged me to make an explosion of my discoveries, I was already resolved to move my residence the following day into town, in a quarter where I should have no dealing with princes. This plan let me spend a more tranquil night, but did not rid me of the pain of having to tremble for a new infidelity.

When I awoke, Manon declared to me that just because I was spending the day in our apartment she did not intend that I should look more unkempt, and that she wanted my hair to be dressed with her own hands. I had a very fine head of hair. This was an amusement she had indulged in several times; but she brought to it more care than I had ever seen her take. To satisfy her, I was obliged to sit in front of her dressing table and put up with all the little devices she imagined for my adornment. In the course of her work she would often turn my face toward her, and, leaning on my shoulders with both hands, gaze at me with avid curiosity. Then, expressing her satisfaction by one or two kisses, she would

make me resume my position and would continue
her work. This trifling kept us busy until dinnertime.
The enjoyment she had taken in it had seemed to
me so natural, and her gaiety smacked so little of
artifice, that, unable to reconcile such apparent constancy with a plan for black treachery, I was several
times tempted to open my heart to her and unburden
myself of a load that was beginning to weigh on me.
But each moment I flattered myself that the revela-
tion would come from her, and I was anticipating a
delicious triumph.

We went back into her boudoir. She set about ad-
justing my hair again, and my indulgence made me
yield to her every wish, when she was notified that
the prince of ... was asking to see her. That name
threw me into a transport of anger.

"What's this!" I exclaimed, pushing her away.
"Who? What prince?"

She made no answer to my questions.

"Show him up," she told the servant coolly; and,
turning toward me:

"Dear lover! You whom I adore," she said in an
enchanting tone, "I ask you for one moment of indulgence. One moment. One single moment. I will
love you for it a thousand times more. I will be
grateful to you for it all my life."

Indignation and surprise tied my tongue. She kept
repeating her entreaties, and I was looking for words
to reject them with disdain. But, hearing the door of
the antechamber open, with one hand she grasped
my hair, which was floating over my shoulders; with
the other she picked up her hand mirror; she used
all her strength to drag me, in this state, as far as the
boudoir door; and, opening it with her knee, she dis-
played to the foreigner, whom the noise seemed to
have halted in the middle of the room, a spectacle
which must have caused him no little astonishment.
I saw a man very well dressed but rather ill-favored.
In the embarrassment into which this scene cast him
he did not fail to make a deep bow. Manon did not

give him time to open his mouth. She held up her
mirror to him:

"See, sir," she said to him, "take a good look at
yourself, and then do me justice. You ask me for
love. Here is the man I love and whom I have sworn
to love all my life. Make the comparison yourself.
If you think you can compete with him for my heart,
then tell me on what basis; for I declare to you
that in the eyes of your very humble servant, all the
princes of Italy are not worth one of the hairs I am
holding."

During this mad speech, which she had apparently
premeditated, I was making futile efforts to get
free; and taking pity on a man of his position, I felt
impelled to make amends for this little outrage by my
civilities. But he recovered himself rather easily, and
his reply, which struck me as a little coarse, made me
lose this inclination.

"Mademoiselle, mademoiselle," he said to her with
a forced smile, "my eyes are indeed opened, and I
find you much less of a novice than I had supposed."

He immediately withdrew without a glance at her,
adding in a lower voice that the women of France
were no better than those of Italy. There was nothing
to invite me, on this occasion, to urge on him a better opinion of the fair sex.

Manon let go of my hair, threw herself into a
chair, and made the room resound with long peals of
laughter. I will not disguise the fact that I was
touched to the bottom of my heart by a sacrifice
which I could attribute only to love. However, the
joke seemed to me excessive. I reproached her for
it. She told me that my rival, after importuning her
for several days at the Bois de Boulogne and making
her guess his feelings by his grimaces, had determined
to make an open declaration of these feelings, accompanied by his name and all his titles, in a letter
which he had had delivered to her by the coachman
who drove her and her friends; that he promised her,
beyond the Alps, a brilliant fortune and eternal ado-

ration; that she had come back to Chaillot with the
resolve of telling me this adventure, but, having had
the idea that we might derive some amusement from
it, she had not been able to resist her fancy; she had
offered the Italian prince, by a flattering reply, the
liberty to come and see her; and she had given herself a further pleasure by making me enter into her
plan without giving me the slightest suspicion of it. I
said not a word to her of the information that had
reached me by another path, and the intoxication of
triumphant love made me approve of everything.[3]

I have noticed all through my life that Heaven has
always chosen, to strike me with its harshest punishments, the time when my fortune seemed to me most
firmly established. I thought myself so happy, with the
friendship of Monsieur de T ... and the love of Manon, that I could not have been made to understand
that I had any new misfortune to fear. However, one
was impending, so disastrous that it reduced me to
the state you saw me in at Pacy and, by degrees, to
extremities so deplorable that you will have difficulty
in believing that my account is true.

One day when we were having Monsieur de T ...
to supper, we heard the noise of a carriage stopping
at the door of the inn. Curiosity made us wish to
know who could be arriving at that hour. We were
told that it was young G ... M ..., that is to say
the son of our cruelest enemy, that old debauchee
who had put me into Saint-Lazare and Manon into the
Hôpital. His name brought the blood to my face.

"It is Heaven that brings him to me," I said to
Monsieur de T ..., "to punish him for his father's
dastardliness. He will not escape me until we have
measured swords."

Monsieur de T ..., who knew him and was
even one of his best friends, tried to give me a different feeling toward him. He assured me that he was

[3] Here ends the episode of the Italian prince, which began
on p. 115. Its insertion into the 1753 edition caused a few
minor changes in the sentences that follow.

a very likable young man, and so incapable of having had any share in his father's act that I would not see him even for a moment without granting him my esteem and wishing to have his. After adding a thousand things to his advantage, he asked me to consent to his going and inviting him to sit with us and share the remainder of our supper. He forestalled the objection of the peril to which it would expose Manon to reveal her abode to the son of our enemy, by protesting on his honor and his good faith that when he came to know us we would have no more zealous defender. I made no difficulty over anything after such assurances.

Monsieur de T... did not bring him in without taking a moment to inform him who we were. He entered with an air that indeed prepossessed us in his favor. He embraced me. We sat down. He admired Manon, myself, everything pertaining to us, and he ate with an appetite that did honor to our supper. When the table was cleared the conversation grew more serious. He lowered his eyes when he spoke to us of the excess his father had gone to against us. He made us the most submissive excuses.

"I cut them short," he said to us, "so as not to revive a memory that fills me with too much shame."

If these excuses were sincere from the start, they became much more so later on, for he had not spent half an hour in conversation with us when I noticed the impression that Manon's charms were making on him. His glances and his manner became more tender by degrees. He let nothing slip out, nevertheless, in his words; but even without any help from jealousy, I had too much experience in love not to discern what came from that source. He kept us company for part of the night and left us only after congratulating himself on making our acquaintances and asking our permission to come again some time and renew the offer of his services. He left in the morning with Monsieur de T..., who joined him in his carriage.

I felt, as I have said, no inclination to jealousy. I had more credulity than ever for Manon's vows. This charming creature was so absolutely mistress of my soul that I had not a single little feeling that was not esteem and love. Far from thinking it a crime for her to have attracted young G ... M ..., I was delighted with the effect of her charms, and I congratulated myself on being loved by a girl whom everyone found lovable. I did not even judge it appropriate to communicate my suspicions to her. We were busy for a few days with the task of having her clothes adjusted and considering whether we could go to the Comédie Française without fear of being recognized. Monsieur de T . . . came back to see us before the end of the week; we consulted him on that. He saw clearly that he had to say yes, to please Manon. We resolved to go there that same evening with him.

However, this resolve could not be carried out; for, having immediately drawn me aside:

"I have been extremely concerned," he said to me, "since I saw you, and the visit I am paying you today is a consequence. G ... M ... loves your mistress. He confided this to me. I am his intimate friend and disposed to serve him in all things; but I am yours no less. I have thought his intentions unjust and condemned them. I would have kept his secret if he intended to use only the ordinary ways to try to please; but he is well informed about Manon's disposition. He has learned, I know not where, that she loves affluence and pleasures; and since he already enjoys a considerable fortune, he has declared to me that he means to tempt her first by a very fat present and the offer of a pension of ten thousand livres. Other things being equal, I would probably have had to do myself much more violence to betray his confidence; but justice has joined friendship in your favor; the more so because, having been the imprudent cause of his passion by bringing him in here, I am obliged to prevent the effects of the harm I have done."

I thanked Monsieur de T . . . for a service of this

importance and confessed to him, with a perfect return of his confidence, that Manon's character was just as G . . . M . . . supposed; that is to say, that she could not endure even the word "poverty."

"However," I said to him, "when it is only a question of more or less, I do not think her capable of abandoning me for another. I am in a position not to let her lack anything, and I count on my fortune growing from day to day. I fear only one thing," I added, "and that is that G . . . M . . . may use the knowledge he has of our address to do us some disservice."

Monsieur de T . . . assured me that I should have no apprehension on that score; that G . . . M . . . was capable of an amorous folly, but not of any baseness; that if he was low enough to commit one, he himself, he who spoke, would be the first to punish him for it and thereby repair the misfortune he had had in giving rise to it.

"I am obliged to you for that feeling," I said, "but the harm would be done and the remedy very uncertain. Thus the wisest course is to forestall it by leaving Chaillot and taking other lodgings."

"Yes," said Monsieur de T . . . ," but you will have trouble in doing that as promptly as would be necessary; for G . . . M . . . is to be here at noon; he told me so yesterday, and that is what led me to come so early to inform you of his intentions. He may arrive at any moment."

Such an urgent warning made me view this matter in a more serious light. Since it seemed impossible to avoid G . . . M . . . 's visit and would no doubt be equally so to keep him from making overtures to Manon, I decided to forewarn her myself about the plan of this new rival. I imagined that, knowing I was informed of the propositions he would make to her and receiving them before my eyes, she would have strength enough to reject them. I disclosed my idea to Monsieur de T . . . , who replied that that was an extremely delicate matter.

"I admit it," I said to him; "but all the reasons a man can have for being sure of a mistress, all these I have for counting on the affection of mine. There is nothing but the magnitude of the offers that could possibly dazzle her; and I have told you, she is innocent of self-interest. She loves her comforts, but she loves me too; and in the state my affairs are in, I cannot believe that she would prefer to me the son of a man who put her in the Hôpital."

In a word, I persisted in my plan, and, drawing Manon aside, I told her candidly all I had just learned.

She thanked me for my good opinion of her and promised me to receive G . . . M . . . 's offers in a way that would rid him of any desire to renew them.

"No," I told her, "you must not irritate him by an affront. He can harm us. But you know well enough, you little devil," I added, laughing, "how to get rid of a disagreeable or importunate lover."

She went on, after pondering a bit:

"A wonderful plan comes to my mind," she exclaimed, "and I am very proud indeed of thinking of it. G . . . M . . . is the son of our cruelest enemy; we must avenge ourselves on the father, not through the son but through his purse. I mean to listen to him, accept his presents, and laugh in his face."

"The plan is a pretty one," I said to her, "but you forget, my poor child, that that is the road that took us straight to the Hôpital."

In vain I pointed out to her the peril of this enterprise; she told me it was only a matter of taking our measures well, and she answered all my objections. Show me a lover who does not blindly enter into all the whims of an adored mistress, and I will acknowledge that I was wrong to yield so easily. The decision was reached to make G . . . M . . . our dupe; and by a bizarre twist of my destiny, it turned out that I became his.

We saw his carriage appear about eleven o'clock. He paid us some very elaborate compliments on the liberty he was taking of coming to dine with us. He

was not surprised to find Monsieur de T . . . , who
had promised him the day before to come too, and
who had pretended some business to excuse himself
from coming in the same carriage. Although there
was not a single one of us who did not bear treachery in his heart, we sat down to table with an air
of mutual confidence and friendship. G . . . M . . .
easily found the chance to declare his feelings to
Manon. I must have seemed to him very little in the
way; for I absented myself on purpose for a few
minutes. I perceived on my return that he had not
been driven to despair by any excess of rigor. He
was in the best humor in the world. I affected to
appear so too; he was laughing inwardly at my simplicity, and I at his. All through the afternoon we provided
a very pleasant scene for one another. I further
arranged for him, before he left, a moment of private
talk with Manon; so that he had reason to congratulate himself on my complaisance as well as on the
good cheer.

As soon as he had climbed into his carriage with
Monsieur de T . . . , Manon ran to me with open
arms and kissed me, bursting with laughter. She repeated his speeches and his propositions to me without changing a word. They came down to this: he
adored her. He wanted to share with her forty thousand livres a year that he already enjoyed, without
counting what he was expecting after the death of
his father. She was to be mistress of his heart and
his fortune; and as a pledge of these benefactions of
his, he was ready to give her a coach, a furnished
house, a maid, three lackeys, and a cook.

"There is a son," I said to Manon, "far more generous than his father. Let's speak in all good faith,"
I added; "doesn't this offer tempt you at all?"

"Me?" she replied, adapting some verses of Racine[4] to her thought:

---

[4] The French of the parody is this:

"Can you suspect *me* of such perfidy?
That odious face before me must I find,
Which always brings the Hôpital to mind?"

"No," I replied, going on with the parody:

"I cannot think, Madame, the Hôpital
Served as Love's dart to print him in your soul."

But a furnished house, with a carriage and three lackeys, is a very seductive dart; and love has few as powerful."

She protested that her heart was mine forever, and that it would never receive any other darts[5] than mine.

MANON
Moi! vous me soupçonnez de cette perfidie?
Moi! je pourrois souffrir un visage odieux,
Qui rappelle toujours l'Hôpital à mes yeux?

DES GRIEUX
J'aurois peine à penser que l'Hôpital, Madame,
Fût un trait dont l'amour l'eût gravé dans votre âme.

The lines parodied are from Racine's *Iphigénie*, Act. 11, scene v, lines 674-682:

ÉRIPHILE
Moi? Vous me soupçonnez de cette perfidie?
Moi, j'aimerois, Madame, un vainqueur furieux
Qui toujours tout sanglant se présente à mes yeux,
Qui la flamme à la main, et de meurtres avide,
Mit en cendres Lesbos . . .
IPHIGÉNIE

                Oui, vous l'aimez, perfide.

Et ces mêmes fureurs que vous me dépeignez,
Ces bras que dans le sang vous avez vus baignés,
Ces morts, cette Lesbos, ces cendres, cette flamme,
Sont les traits dont l'amour l'a gravé dans votre âme . . .

----

[5] The French word for "darts" here and above is *traits*, which also means "features"; thus Manon may also mean that she will take no one's features into her heart but those of Des Grieux.

"The promises he made me," she said, "are a spur to vengeance rather than a dart of love."

I asked her whether it was her plan to accept the house and the carriage. She replied that she was out only for his money. The difficulty was to get one without the other. We resolved to wait for the entire explanation of G...M...'s plan in a letter he had promised to write her. She received it in fact the next morning from a lackey out of livery who very adroitly procured an opportunity to speak to her without witnesses. She told him to wait for her answer, and she came straightway to bring me his letter. We opened it together. Besides the common-places of tender affection, it contained the details of my rival's promises. He spared no expense. He pledged himself to count out to her ten thousand francs when she took possession of the house, and to make up the diminutions of that sum in such wise that she would always have it on front of her in ready cash. The day of the inauguration was not too far off: he asked for only two days for the preparations, and he indicated the name of the street and of the house, where he promised to be waiting for her on the afternoon of the second day, if she could slip out of my hands. That was the only point about which he conjured her to relieve his anxiety; he seemed sure of all the rest; but he added that if she foresaw any difficulty in escaping me, he would find means to make her flight easy.

G...M... was shrewder than his father He wanted to hold his prey before counting out his money. We deliberated over the course that Manon was to take. I made still more efforts to put the undertaking out of her mind, and I pointed out all its dangers to her. Nothing could shake her resolution.

She made a short reply to G...M...to assure him that she would find no difficulty in going to Paris on the appointed day and that he could expect her with certainty. We then decided that I should leave

immediately to go and rent new lodgings in some
village on the other side of Paris, and transport our
few belongings with me; that the next afternoon, which
was the time of her assignation, she should go to
Paris early; that after receiving G . . . M . . . 's presents she should entreat him urgently to take her to
the Comédie; that she should take with her all of the
sum that she could carry and entrust the rest to my
valet, whom she intended to take with her. This was
still the same one who had delivered her from the
Hôpital and who was devotedly attached to us. I was
to be in a cab at the entrance to the Rue Saint-André-
des-Arcs[6] and leave it there about seven o'clock to
go up in the darkness to the doorway of the theater.
Manon promised me to invent pretexts for leaving
her box for a moment, and use that moment to come
down and join me. The rest would be easy to carry
out. We would have regained my cab in a moment
and have left Paris by the Faubourg Saint-Antoine,
which was the way to our new lodgings.

This plan, absurd as it was, seemed to us rather
well arranged. But at bottom it was mad imprudence
to imagine that even if it had succeeded in the most
fortunate possible way, we could ever have sheltered
ourselves from pursuit. However, we exposed ourselves with the rashest confidence. Manon left with
Marcel; that was the name of our valet. It was with
grief that I saw her leave. I said to her as I kissed
her:

"Manon, don't deceive me; will you be faithful to
me?"

She complained tenderly of my mistrust and renewed all her vows to me.

She reckoned on arriving in Paris about three
o'clock. I left after her. I went and moped for the
rest of the afternoon in the Café de Feré near the

6 Now written Saint-André-des-Arts; an old street in the
Latin quarter near the Seine and near the old Comédie
Française.

Pont Saint-Michel. I stayed there until nightfall. Then I left to take a cab, which I posted, according to our plan, at the entrance of the Rue Saint-André-des-Arcs; next I went to the door of the theater on foot. I was surprised not to find Marcel, who was supposed to wait for me there. I took patience for an hour, lost in a crowd of lackeys, my eyes on all the passers-by. Finally, seven o'clock having struck without my having perceived anything relating to our plans, I bought a ticket to the pit, to go and see if I could catch a glimpse of Manon and G . . . M . . . in the boxes. Neither one was there. I went back to the door, where I spent another quarter of an hour, transported with impatience and anxiety. Having seen nothing, I returned to my cab without being able to come to the slightest decision. The coachman, seeing me, came a few steps toward me and said, with a mysterious air, that a pretty young lady had been waiting an hour for me in the carriage; that she had asked for me in terms that he had recognized, and, having learned that I was due to come back, she had said she would wait for me without impatience.

I imagined immediately that it was Manon. I approached. But I saw a pretty little face, which was not hers. It was a stranger, who first asked me if she did not have the honor of speaking to the Chevalier des Grieux. I told her that that was my name.

"I have a letter to deliver to you," she went on, "which will inform you of the reason that brings me and through what connection I have the advantage of knowing your name."

I asked her to give me the time to read it in a nearby tavern. She wanted to come with me, and advised me to ask for a private room.

"Whom is this letter from?" I asked her as we went upstairs.

She set me to reading it. I recognized Manon's hand. This is about what she told me:

G . . . M . . . had received her with a politeness and a magnificence beyond her wildest dreams. He

had loaded her with presents. He made her glimpse
the life of a queen. She assured me nevertheless that
she was not forgetting me in this new splendor; but
that having been unable to make G... M... consent to take her to the Comédie that evening, she put
off to another day the pleasure of seeing me; and
that to console me a bit for the pain she foresaw
this news might cause me, she had managed to procure me one of the prettiest girls in Paris, who would
be the bearer of her note. *Signed:* "Your faithful love,
MANON LESCAUT."

There was something so cruel and so insulting to
me in this letter, that, suspended for some time between anger and grief, I undertook to make an effort
to forget my ungrateful and forsworn mistress for
eternity. I cast my eyes on the girl in front of me.
She was extremely pretty; and I could have wished
that she had been enough so to make me forsworn
and faithless in my turn. But I did not find in her
those delicate languishing eyes, that divine bearing,
that complexion composed by love itself, in fine that
inexhaustible wealth of charms that nature had lavished on the perfidious Manon.

"No, no," I said to her, looking away from her,
"the ingrate who sent you knew very well that she
was sending you on a useless errand. Go back to
her and tell her from me to enjoy her crime, and
enjoy it, if she can, without remorse. I abandon her
never to return, and at the same time I renounce
all women, who cannot be as attractive as she and
who are no doubt just as low and as faithless."

I was then on the point of going downstairs and
away, with no further claims on Manon; and as the
deadly jealousy that was rending my heart disguised
itself as a dreary and somber tranquillity, I thought
I was all the closer to my cure because I felt none
of those violent emotions that had agitated me on
similar occasions. Alas! I was the dupe of love, just
as much as I thought I was of G... M... and
Manon.

This girl, who had brought me the letter, seeing me ready to go downstairs, asked me what message I wanted her to take back, then, to Monsieur de G . . . M . . . and the lady who was with him. At this question, I went back into the room; and through a change unbelievable to those who have never felt violent passions, I found myself all of a sudden, from the tranquillity I thought I was in, transported into a terrible fury.

"Go," I told her, "report to the traitor G . . . M . . . and his perfidious mistress the despair into which your accursed letter has cast me; but tell them that they will not laugh over it for long, and that I will stab them both to death with my own hand."

I threw myself on a chair. My hat fell to the floor on one side, and my cane on the other. Two streams of bitter tears began to flow from my eyes. The fit of rage that I had just experienced changed to profound grief. I did nothing but weep, heaving groans and sighs.

"Come here, my child, come here," I exclaimed, addressing the girl. "Come here, since it is you who are sent to console me. Tell me whether you know any consolations against rage and despair, against the wish to take one's own life after killing two traitors who do not deserve to live. Yes, come here," I went on, seeing that she was taking a few timid and uncertain steps toward me. "Come and dry my tears; come and restore peace to my heart, come and tell me that you love me, so that I may become accustomed to being loved by someone other than my faithless girl. You are pretty, I may perhaps be able to love you in return."

This poor child, who was no more than sixteen or seventeen, and who seemed to have more modesty than most of her kind, was extraordinarily surprised at so strange a scene. She came up nevertheless and gave me a few caresses, but I repulsed her immediately, pushing her away with my hands.

"What do you want of me?" I asked her. "Ah!

You are a woman, you are of a sex which I detest and which I can no longer endure. The sweetness of your face threatens me with yet another betrayal! Go away and leave me alone."

She curtsied to me without daring to say anything, and turned to leave. I called out to her to stop.

"But at least tell me," I went on, "why, how, and with what purpose you were sent here. How did you discover my name and the place where you could find me?"

She told me that she had known Monsieur de G... M... for a long time; that he had sent for her at five o'clock, and, following the lackey who had notified her, she had gone to a big house where she had found him playing piquet with a pretty lady; that they had both commissioned her to give me the letter she had brought me, after telling her that she would find me in a carriage at the end of the Rue Saint-André. I asked her whether they had said anything more to her. She answered me, blushing, that they had led her to hope that I would take her to keep me company.

"They tricked you," I said to her; "my poor girl, they tricked you. You are a woman. You need a man. But you need one who is rich and happy, and it is not here that you can find him. Go back, go back to Monsieur de G... M.... He has all it takes to be loved by beautiful women. He has furnished houses and retinues to give away. As for me, who have nothing to offer but love and constancy, women despise my misery and make sport of my simplicity."

I added a thousand things, either violent or sad, according as the passions that agitated me alternately yielded or got the upper hand. However, by dint of tormenting me, my transports diminished enough to give way to a few reflections. I compared this last misfortune with those of the same kind I had already endured, and I did not find that there was more reason to despair than in the first ones. I knew Manon;

why distress myself so over a mishap that I should have foreseen? Why not rather concern myself with seeking a remedy? There was still time. I should at least not spare my pains if I did not want to have to reproach myself with having contributed, by my negligence, to my own sorrows. Thereupon I set myself to considering all the means that might open me a road to hope.

To undertake to snatch her from the hands of G... M... by violence was a desperate course, which was fit only to ruin me and which had not the slightest likelihood of success. But it seemed to me that if I could have procured the least bit of talk with her I would infallibly have won some sway over her heart. I knew all its sensibilities so well! I was so sure of her love for me! Even this bizarre action of sending me a pretty girl to console me came, I would have bet, from her imagination, and was an effect of her compassion for my griefs. I resolved to use all my ingenuity to see her. Among a quantity of courses that I considered one after the other, I settled on this one. Monsieur de T . . . had begun to do me services with too much affection to leave me the slightest doubt of his sincerity and zeal. I proposed to go and see him right away and prevail upon him to send for G... M... on the pretext of important business. I needed only half an hour to talk to Manon. My plan was to have myself shown right into her room, and I thought this would be easy for me in G...M...'s absence.

This resolution having made me calmer, I liberally paid the girl, who was still with me; and to remove her desire to return to those who had sent her, I took her address, giving her the hope that I would go and spend the night with her. I climbed into my cab and had myself driven at high speed to Monsieur de T . . .'s. I was fortunate enough to find him in. I had been worried about that on the way. A few words acquainted him with my woes and the service I had come to ask of him. He was so astounded to learn

that G . . . M . . . had been able to seduce Manon
that, not knowing that I myself had played a part in
my mishap, he generously offered to assemble all his
friends and use their arms and swords to deliver my
mistress I made him understand that such an out-
break could be pernicious for Manon and me.

"Let us save our blood," I said to him, "for a last
resort. I am thinking about a milder course which I
hope will be no less successful."

He pledged himself unreservedly to do anything I
asked of him; and when I repeated that all I had in
mind was for him to get word to G . . . M . . . that
he had something to talk to him about, and to keep
him out of the house for an hour or two, he left
with me immediately to do as I wished.

We cast about for an expedient he could use to
detain him so long. I advised him first to write him
a simple note, dated from a tavern, in which he would
ask him to come there immediately about a matter
so important that it could brook no delay.

"I shall observe," I added, "the moment he leaves,
and I shall gain admittance to the house without difficulty, being known there only to Manon and to Marcel, who is my valet. As for you, who during this
time will be with G . . . M . . . , you can tell him
this important matter you want to speak to him about
is a need for money; that you have just lost yours at
gambling, and have staked much more on your word,
with the same bad luck. He will need time to take you
to his strongbox, and I shall have enough to carry
out my plan."

Monsieur de T . . . followed this arrangement point
for point. I left him in a tavern, where he promptly
wrote his letter. I went and stationed myself a few
steps from Manon's house. I saw the bearer of the message arrive and G . . . M . . . go out on foot a moment later, followed by a lackey. Having left him time
to get far enough away from the street, I went up to
the door of my faithless love; and in spite of all my
anger, I knocked with the respect one feels for a

temple. Fortunately it was Marcel who came and opened the door. I signaled to him to be silent. Although I had nothing to fear from the other servants, I asked him in a very low voice if he could take me to the room where Manon was without my being observed. He told me that was easy by going quietly up the main stairs.

"Then let's go promptly," I said to him, "and while I am there, try to keep anyone from coming up."

I entered her room without any obstacle. Manon was busy reading. This was where I had occasion to marvel at the character of this strange girl. Far from being frightened and appearing timid when she saw me, she showed only those slight signs of surprise which we cannot master at the sight of a person we think is far away.

"Ah! It's you, my love," she said, coming and kissing me with her usual tenderness. "Good Lord! How bold you are! Who would have expected you in this place today?"

I freed myself from her arms, and far from responding to her caresses, I pushed her off with disdain and took two or three steps backward to get away from her. This movement did not fail to disconcert her. She remained in the position she was in, and she cast her eyes on me, changing color. I was at bottom so enchanted to see her again that even with so many just reasons for anger I hardly had the strength to open my mouth to reproach her. However, my heart was bleeding from the cruel outrage she had done me. I recalled it vividly to my memory, to excite my resentment; and I tried to make my eyes shine with another fire than that of love. Since I remained for some time in silence and she noticed my agitation, I saw her tremble, apparently as a result of fear. I could not endure this sight.

"Ah! Manon," I said to her in a tender tone, "faithless and forsworn Manon! Where shall I begin my complaint? I see you pale and trembling, and I am still so sensible to the slightest of your sufferings that

I am afraid of afflicting you too much by my reproaches. But, Manon, I tell you: my heart is pierced
with the pain of your betrayal. Those are blows you
do not deal to a lover unless you have resolved on
his death. This is the third time, Manon; I have counted them well; it is impossible for that to be forgotten. It is for you to consider, right now, what
course you want to take; for my sad heart is no
longer proof against such cruel treatment. I can feel
it succumbing and ready to break with grief. I
cannot go on," I added, sinking into a chair; "I hardly have the strength to speak or stand."

She did not answer me; but when I was seated, she
knelt down and leaned her head on my knees, hiding
her face in my hands. In a moment I felt them wet
with her tears. Ye Gods! With what emotions was
I not torn!

"Ah! Manon, Manon," I went on with a sigh, "it is
very late to offer me tears, when you have caused
my death. You are putting on a sadness you cannot
possibly feel. The greatest of your woes, doubtless, is
my presence, which has always been troublesome to
your pleasures. Open your eyes, see who I am; one
does not shed such tender tears for a wretch whom
one has betrayed and is abandoning cruelly."

She kept kissing my hands, without changing her
position.

"Inconstant Manon," I went on again, "thankless and
faithless girl, where are your promises and your
vows? Ever fickle and cruel mistress, what have you
done with that love that you were swearing to me
even today? Oh, just Heavens!" I added. "Is it thus
that someone faithless laughs at you, after having
called you to witness such sacred oaths? So it is per-
jury that is rewarded! Despair and abandonment are
the wages of constancy and fidelity."

These words were accompanied by such a bitter
meditation that I let a few tears escape me in spite of
myself. Manon noticed this by the change in my
voice. At last she broke the silence.

"I certainly must be guilty," she said to me sadly, "since I have succeeded in causing you so much pain and emotion; but may Heaven punish me if I thought I was or if I had any idea of becoming so!"

This statement seemed to me so lacking in sense and good faith that I could not resist a sharp burst of anger.

"What horrible dissimulation!" I cried. "I see better than ever that you are nothing but a perfidious hussy. It is now that I know your wretched character. Farewell, vile creature," I went on, rising, "I would rather die a thousand deaths than have anything to do with you from now on. May Heaven punish *me* if I ever honor you with the slightest glance! Stay with your new lover, love him, detest me, renounce honor and good sense; it makes me laugh, it's all the same to me."

She was so terrified by this outburst that, remaining on her knees beside the chair I had left, she gazed at me trembling and without daring to breathe. I took a few steps toward the door, turning my head and keeping my eyes fixed on her. But I would have had to have lost all human feelings to harden myself against so many charms. I was so far from having that barbaric strength that, passing suddenly to the opposite extreme, I went back toward her, or rather I flung myself toward her, without deliberation. I took her in my arms. I gave her a thousand tender kisses. I begged her pardon for my fury. I confessed that I was a brute, that I did not deserve the happiness of being loved by a girl like her. I got her to sit down, and, throwing myself in turn on my knees, I entreated her to listen to me in that posture. All the most respectful and tender feelings that a submissive and passionate lover can imagine, I there epitomized in a few words in my excuses. I asked her as a mercy to say that she forgave me. She dropped her arms around my neck, saying that it was she who needed my kindness in order to make me forget the griefs she caused me, and that she was

beginning to fear with reason that I would not like what
she had to say to me in justifying herself.

"I!" I interrupted immediately. "Ah! I ask no justi-
fication. I approve of all you have done. It is not
for me to demand your reasons for your conduct; I
am only too satisfied, too happy, if my dear Manon
does not take from me the tenderness of her heart!
But," I went on, thinking of the state of my lot, "all-
powerful Manon, you who create my joys and my
sorrows as you wish, after satisfying you by my hu-
miliations and the signs of my repentance, shall I not
be allowed to tell you of my sadness and my griefs?
Am I to learn from you what is to become of me
today, and whether it is past recall that you are going to sign my death sentence by spending the night
with my rival?"

She was some time meditating her reply.

"My own Chevalier," she said, resuming a calm
manner, "if you had explained yourself that clearly
from the first, you would have spared yourself much
disturbance and me a very distressing scene. Since
your grief comes only from your jealousy, I would
have cured it by offering to follow you this instant
to the end of the world. But I supposed it was the
letter I wrote you under Monsieur de G . . . M . . .'s
eyes, and the girl we sent you, that were causing
your chagrin. I thought you might have regarded my
letter as a mockery and that girl—imagining that she
had gone to see you at my behest—as a declaration
that I was giving you up and attaching myself to
G . . . M . . . . It was this thought that suddenly
plunged me into consternation; for no matter how innocent I was, it struck me, on thinking about it, that
the appearances were not in my favor. However,"
she went on, "I want you to be my judge, after I
have explained to you the truth of the matter."

She then told me all that had happened to her
since she had found G . . . M . . . waiting for her in
the place where we now were. He had indeed received
her like the greatest princess in the world. He had

shown her all the suites, which were admirably taste-
ful and neat. He had counted out ten thousand livres
to her in his study, and had added to that some
jewels, among them the pearl necklace and bracelets
that she had already gotten from his father. He had
taken her from there into a salon that she had not
yet seen, where she had found an exquisite collation.
He had had her waited on by the new servants that
he had taken on for her, ordering them to consider
her henceforth as their mistress; finally he had shown
her the carriage, the horses, and all the rest of his
presents; after which he had proposed a game of
cards while waiting for supper.

"I admit," she went on, "that I was struck by this
magnificence. I reflected that it would be a pity to
deprive ourselves all at once of so many riches by
contenting myself with carrying off the ten thousand
francs and the jewels; that it was a ready-made fortune for you and me, and that we could live agree-
ably at G . . . M . . . 's expense. Instead of proposing
the Comédie to him, I took it into my head to sound
him out about you in order to anticipate what facili-
ties we should have for seeing each other, supposing
my plan was carried out. I found him very easy to
deal with. He asked me what I thought of you and
whether I had not had some regret at leaving you. I
told him that you were so attractive and had always
treated me so honorably that it would not be natural
that I could hate you. He confessed that you had
merit and that he had felt impelled to desire your
friendship. He wanted to know how I thought you
would take my leaving, especially when you should
come to know that I was in his hands. I answered
that the date of our love was already so old that it
had had time to cool a little, that furthermore you
were not very well off, and that you might regard
the loss of me as no great misfortune, since it would
unburden you of a load that was weighing on your
arms.

"I added that being completely convinced that you

would behave peacefully, I had made no difficulty
about telling you that I was coming to Paris on some
errands; that you had consented, and, having come
in yourself, you had not appeared very worried when
I left you. 'If I thought,' he said to me, 'that he
would be minded to live on good terms with me,
I would be the first to offer him my services and my
compliments.' I assured him that, from my knowledge
of your character, I had no doubt that you would
reply nicely, especially, I said to him, if he could
serve you in your affairs, which had been in very
poor shape since you had been on bad terms with
your family. He interrupted me to protest that he
would render you all the services that depended on
him; and that if you even wanted to embark upon
another love, he would procure you a pretty mistress, whom he had left to attach himself to me.

"I applauded his idea," she added, "to forestall all
his suspicions the more perfectly; and, confirming myself more and more in my plan, I wished only to be
able to find a way to inform you of it, for fear you
might be too alarmed when you saw that I missed
our rendezvous. It was with that in view that I proposed he send you this new mistress that very evening, so I would have an occasion for writing you;
I was obliged to have recourse to this stratagem, because I could not hope that he would leave me free
for a moment. He laughed at my proposition. He
called his lackey, and having asked him whether he
could find his former mistress immediately, he sent
him this way and that to look for her. He imagined
that it was at Chaillot that she should go and find
you; but I told him that on leaving you I had promised to meet you at the Comédie; or if some reason
kept me from going there, you had undertaken to
wait for me in a carriage at the end of the Rue Saint-
André; that consequently it was better to send your
new mistress to you there, were it only to keep you
from freezing there all night. I further told him it
was best that I should write you a line to tell you

about this exchange, which you would have trouble in understanding without that. He consented to this; but I was obliged to write in his presence, and I took good care not to explain myself too openly in my letter.

"That," Manon added, "is the way things happened. I am disguising nothing to you about either my conduct or my plans. The girl came, I found her pretty; and since I had no doubt that my absence would cause you grief, it was sincerely that I wished she might serve to dispel your boredom for a few moments; for the fidelity I wish from you is that of the heart. I would have been delighted to be able to send you Marcel; but I could not get a moment to tell him what I wanted to let you know."

She concluded her story at last by telling me of G . . . M . . . 's embarrassment on receiving Monsieur de T . . . 's note.

"He debated," she told me, "whether he should leave me, and he assured me that he would be back without delay. That is why it is not without anxiety that I see you here, and why I showed surprise when you arrived."

I listened to this speech with much patience. I certainly found in it a quantity of points that were cruel and mortifying for me; for the deliberateness of her infidelity was so clear that she had not even taken the trouble to disguise it to me. She could not hope that G . . . M . . . would leave her alone all night, like a vestal virgin. So it was with him that she intended to spend it. What an admission, for a lover! However, I recognized that I was in part the cause of her fault, by the knowledge I had given her in the first place of the feelings G . . . M . . . had for her and by my complaisance in joining blindly in the rash plan of her adventure. Besides, by a natural trait of my particular make-up, I was touched by the ingenuousness of her story and by the good open manner in which she told me even the circumstances at which I was most offended. She sins without malice, I said to myself. She is frivolous and imprudent; but she is straight and sincere. Add to this the fact that love alone was sufficient to make me close my eyes to all her faults. I was only too satisfied with the hope of taking her away from my rival that very evening. Nevertheless I said to her:

"And the night—with whom would you have spent it?"

This question, which I asked her sadly, embarrassed her. She answered me only with uncompleted "if's" and "but's." I had pity on her plight and, breaking off this subject, I told her, naturally, that I expected her to follow me that instant.

"I am willing," she said to me, "but then you don't approve of my plan?"

"Hah! Isn't it enough," I retorted, "that I approve of everything you have done up to now?"

"What! We won't even take the ten thousand francs?" she replied. "He gave them to me. They're mine."

I advised her to leave everything behind and think only of getting away from there promptly; for although I had been with her barely a half hour, I feared the return of G . . . M . . . . However, she insisted so urgently on my consenting not to leave empty-handed that I thought I ought to grant her something after obtaining so much from her.

During the time that we were preparing to leave I heard a knock on the street door. I had no doubt whatever that it was G . . . M . . . ; and in the confusion into which this thought cast me, I told Manon that he was a dead man if he appeared. Indeed, I had not recovered enough from my emotions to control myself if I saw him. Marcel ended my anxiety by bringing me a note that he had accepted for me at the door. It was from Monsieur de T . . . . It informed me that since G . . . M . . . had gone home to get some money for him, he was taking advantage of his absence to communicate a very amusing idea to me: that it seemed to him I could not avenge

myself more pleasantly on my rival than by eating
his supper and sleeping, that very night, in the bed
he was hoping to occupy with my mistress; that this
seemed to him easy enough if I could assure myself
of three or four men with enough resolution to detain G . . . M . . . in the street and enough fidelity to
keep their eye on him until the morrow; that for his
part, he promised to keep him busy for another hour
at least with reasons which he held in readiness for
his return.

I showed Manon this note and told her what ruse
I had used to gain admittance freely to her room.
My stratagem and that of Monsieur de T . . . seemed
admirable to her. We laughed about them to our
hearts' content for a few moments. But when I spoke
of the latter as a joke, I was surprised that she insisted on proposing it to me seriously as something
the thought of which delighted her. In vain did I ask
her where she expected me to find, all of a sudden,
some people fit to detain G . . . M . . . and guard
him faithfully. She said we must at least try, since
Monsieur de T . . . guaranteed us another hour; and
by way of answer to my other objections, she said I
was playing the tyrant and showing no indulgence
toward her. She thought this the prettiest plan in
the world.

"You shall have his place at supper," she told
me, "you shall sleep between his sheets, and tomorrow very early you shall make off with his mistress
and his money. You will be well avenged on father
and son."

I yielded to her entreaties, despite the secret stir-
rings of my heart, which seemed to forebode a miserable catastrophe. I went out with the intention of
asking two or three guardsmen, whom I knew
through Lescaut, to undertake the task of detaining
G . . . M . . . . I found only one at home, but he was
an enterprising man who had no sooner learned what
was afoot than he assured me of a successful result:
he asked me for only ten pistoles to reward three

soldiers in the guards whom he resolved to employ,
placing himself at their head. I begged him to lose no
time. He got them together in less than a quarter of
an hour. I was waiting for him at his house; and
when he was back with his associates I took him myself to the corner of a street by which G . . . M . . .
must necessarily pass to return to the one Manon
lived on. I recommended to him not to mistreat him,
but to guard him so closely until seven in the morning that I could be sure he would not escape. He
said that his plan was to take him to his own room
and make him undress or even lie down in his bed,
while he and his three bravoes would spend the night
drinking and playing cards.

I stayed with them until the moment I saw G . . .
M . . . appear; and I then withdrew a few steps into
a dark recess to witness such an extraordinary scene.
The guardsman addressed him, pistol in hand, and
explained to him civilly that he had no designs on
either his money or his life; but that if he made
any difficulty over following him or gave the slightest outcry, he would blow his brains out. G . . .
M . . ., seeing him supported by three soldiers, and
no doubt fearing to get the full blast of the pistol,
made no resistance. I saw him led away like a lamb.

I went back immediately to Manon's; and to remove
any suspicion from the servants' minds, I said to
her as I came in that she was not to wait for Monsieur de G . . . M . . . for supper; that important business had come up which detained him in spite of
himself, and that he had asked me to come and
make his excuses to her and have supper with her,
which I regarded as a great favor with so beautiful
a lady. She very adroitly seconded my plan. We sat
down to table. We assumed a serious air as long as
the servants remained waiting on us. Finally, having
dismissed them, we spent one of the most charming
evenings of our life. I secretly ordered Marcel to get
a cabby and tell him to be at the door the next
morning before six. I pretended to leave Manon

about midnight; but having returned quietly with the help of Marcel, I made ready to occupy G . . . M . . .'s bed, as I had filled his place at table.

During this time our evil genius was working out our downfall. We were in the ecstasy of pleasure, and the sword was hanging over our heads. The thread that held it up was about to break. But to give a better understanding of all the circumstances of our ruin, I must clarify the cause.

G . . . M . . . had been followed by a lackey when he was held up by the guardsman. This fellow, frightened at his master's adventure, fled back the way he had come; and the first step he took to rescue him was to go and inform old G . . . M . . . of what had just happened. Such distressing news could not fail to alarm him greatly. He had only that one son, and his reactions were extremely lively for his age. He wanted to know first from the lackey everything his son had done that afternoon: whether he had had a quarrel with anyone, whether he had taken part in someone else's altercation, whether he had been in any dubious house. The lackey, who supposed his master to be in the utmost danger and imagined he should hold back nothing in order to get help to him, disclosed everything he knew about his love for Manon and the expense he had incurred for her, the way he had spent the afternoon in his house until about nine o'clock, his departure, and the mishap on his way back. This was enough to make the old man suspect that his son's affair was a love quarrel. Although it was at least half past ten in the evening, he did not hesitate to call on the Lieutenant General of Police at once. He asked him to give special orders to all the squads of the watch; and having requested one of these to accompany him, he himself hastened to the street where his son had been held up; he searched every place in town where he hoped he might find him; and having been unable to pick up his traces, he finally had himself taken to his mistress' house, to which he imagined he might have returned.

I was about to get into bed when he arrived. The door to the bedroom being closed, I heard none of the knocking on the street door; but he entered the house, followed by two archers, and, having vainly sought information about what had become of his son, he decided to see his mistress to get some light on the matter from her.

He comes upstairs to our suite, still accompanied by his archers. We were ready to go to bed; he opens the door, and freezes our blood at the sight of him.

"Oh God! It's old G... M...," I exclaim to Manon.

I leap for my sword; unfortunately it was entangled in my sword belt. The archers, who saw my move, came up immediately and seized it from me. A man in his nightshirt is helpless. They took from me all means of defense.

G... M..., though discomposed by this spectacle, did not take long to recognize me. He placed Manon even more easily.

"Is this an illusion?" he said to us gravely. "Do I not see the Chevalier des Grieux and Manon Lescaut?"

I was so enraged with shame and grief that I made no reply. For some time he seemed to be turning over various thoughts in his mind; and as if they had suddenly kindled his anger, he addressed me and exclaimed:

"Ah! You wretch, I am sure you have killed my son!"

This insult stung me to the quick.

"You old villain," I retorted proudly, "if I had had anyone in your family to kill, you're the one I would have started with."

"Hold him tight," he said to the archers. "He has got to give me news of my son; I'll have him hanged tomorrow if he does not tell me right now what he has done with him."

"You will have me hanged?" I replied. "You wretch! It is the likes of you that will be found on the gallows. Know that my blood is nobler and purer than yours. Yes," I added, "I know what has happened to your son; and if you irritate me further I will have him strangled before morning, and I promise you the same fate after him."

I committed an imprudence in confessing to him that I knew where his son was; but excess of anger made me perpetrate this indiscretion. He immediately called five or six other archers who were waiting at the door and ordered them to lay hold of all the servants in the house.

"Aha! Sir Chevalier," he went on in a mocking tone, "you know where my son is and you will have him strangled, you say? Rest assured that we will set this matter to rights."

Immediately I sensed the blunder I had committed. He went up to Manon, who was sitting on the bed weeping; he paid her a few ironic gallantries about her dominion over father and son and the fine use she put it to. That lecherous old monster tried to take a few liberties with her.

"Take care you don't touch her!" I cried, "or there would be nothing sacred that could save you from my hands."

He went out, leaving three archers in the room, whom he ordered to have us put on our clothes promptly.

I do not know what his plans were for us then. Perhaps we would have obtained our freedom by informing him where his son was. I was debating, as I dressed, whether that was not the best course. But if this was his disposition when he left the room, it was very changed when he came back in. He had gone and questioned Manon's servants, whom the archers had arrested. He could not learn anything from those she had received from his son; but when he found out that Marcel had served us before, he resolved to make him talk, intimidating him by threats.

He was a faithful lad, but simple and crude. The
memory of what he had done at the Hôpital to deliver Manon, combined with the terror that G . . . M . . .
inspired in him, made so great an impression on his
feeble wits that he imagined they were going to take
him to the gallows or the wheel. He promised to reveal everything that had come to his knowledge if
they would spare his life. On the strength of this
G . . . M . . . convinced himself that there was something more serious and criminal in our affairs than he
had hitherto had reason to suppose. He offered Marcel not only his life but also rewards for his confes-
sion.

That poor creature informed him of part of our
plan, about which we had had no hesitation to talk in
front of him, because he was to have been somewhat
involved in it. It is true that he was entirely unaware
of the changes we had made in this in Paris; but he
had been informed, when we left Chaillot, of the
plan of the undertaking and the part he was to play.
So he declared to him that our aim was to dupe his
son and that Manon was to receive, or had already received, ten thousand francs, which, according to our
plan, would never return to the heirs of the house
of G . . . M . . . .

After this discovery the old man, in a rage, came
back up abruptly into our room. He passed on without speaking into the boudoir, where he had no trouble in finding the money and the jewels. He came
back to us with his face inflamed, and, showing us
what he was pleased to call our loot, he loaded us
with insulting reproaches. He showed Manon the
pearl necklace and bracelets from close up.

"Do you recognize them?" he said to her with a
mocking smile. "This was not the first time you had
seen them. The same ones, on my word! They were
to your taste, my beauty; I can easily believe it. The
poor children!" he added. "They are quite attractive,
indeed, both of them; but they are a bit knavish."

My heart was bursting with rage at this insulting

speech. To be free for one moment I would have given . . . Just Heavens! What would I not have given! Finally I made a violent effort with myself and said to him, with a moderation that was only a refinement of fury:

"Sir, let's end this insolent mockery. What is your plan? Come now, what do you intend to do with us?"

"My plan, Sir Chevalier," he replied, "is for us all to go at once to the Châtelet.[7] Tomorrow is another day; we shall have more light on our affairs, and I hope you will finally grant me the boon of telling me where my son is."

I understood, without many reflections, that it was a terribly serious thing for us to be once locked up in the Châtelet. Trembling, I foresaw all its dangers. In spite of all my pride, I recognized that I must bow beneath the weight of my lot and flatter my cruelest enemy to get something out of him by submission. I begged him in a civil tone to listen to me for a moment.

"I can judge myself, sir," I said to him. "I confess that youth has made me commit great faults and that you are wounded enough by them to bring a complaint. But if you know the power of love; if you can judge what an unfortunate young man suffers when everything he loves is taken away from him, you may find me forgivable for having sought the pleasure of a bit of revenge, or at least you will believe that I am punished enough by the affront I have just received. There is no need of prison or torture to force me to reveal to you where your son is. He is in a safe place. My purpose was not to harm him nor to offend you. I am ready to give you the name of the place where he is peacefully spending the night, if you do me the mercy of granting us our freedom."

That old tiger, far from being touched by my en-

---

[7] The Petit Châtelet, once a fortress defending the bridge leading to the Cité, was in Prévost's time a prison for minor criminals.

treaty, turned his back on me, laughing. He merely let out a few words to give me to understand that he knew our plan all the way back to the beginning. As far as his son was concerned, he added brutally that he would be found all right, since I had not murdered him.

"Take them to the Petit Châtelet," he said to the archers, "and take care that the Chevalier does not escape. He is a tricky one, who already got out of Saint-Lazare."

He went out and left me in the state that you can imagine.

"O Heaven!" I cried. "I shall receive with submission all the blows that come from your hand; but for a miserable scoundrel to have the power to treat me with such tyranny—that is what reduces me to the depths of despair."

The archers asked us not to keep them waiting any longer. They had a coach at the door. I gave Manon my hand coming downstairs.

"Come, my dear queen," I said to her, "come and submit to the full rigor of our lot. Perhaps it will please Heaven some day to make us happier."

We left in the same coach. She came into my arms. I had not heard her utter a word from the first moment that G... M... arrived; but, once alone with me, she told me a thousand loving things, reproaching herself for being the cause of my misfortune. I assured her that I would never complain of my lot as long as she should not stop loving me.

"I am not the one to be pitied," I went on. "A few months in prison do not frighten me at all, and I shall always prefer the Châtelet to Saint-Lazare. But it is for you, my dearest soul, that my heart grieves. What a fate for so charming a creature! How, Heaven, can you treat the most perfect of your works with so much rigor? Why were we not both born with qualities in keeping with our wretched lot? We were endowed with intelligence, taste, feelings. Alas! What a sad use we are making of them, while so many base

souls, worthy of our lot, enjoy all the favors of fortune!"

These reflections pierced me with grief; but this was
nothing in comparison with those that concerned the
future, for I was sick with fear for Manon. She had
already been at the Hôpital; and even if she had left
it by the front door, I knew that relapses of this sort
had extremely dangerous consequences. I would have
liked to express my fears to her. I was apprehensive
of arousing too many in her. I trembled for her, without daring to warn her of the danger, and I was sighing as I embraced her so as to assure her at least of my
love, which was almost the only feeling that I dared
express.

"Manon," I said to her, "tell me sincerely: will you
love me always?"

She answered that she was very unhappy that I
could doubt it.

"Well," I went on, "I do not doubt it, and with that
assurance I am willing to defy all our enemies. I
shall use my family to get out of the Châtelet; and
all my blood will be of no use to me if I do not
get you out as soon as I am free."

We arrived at the prison. We were each put in a
separate place. This blow was the less hard because
I had foreseen it. I commended Manon to the warder,
informing him that I was a man of some distinction
and promising him a considerable reward. I embraced
my dear mistress before leaving her. I conjured her not
to distress herself too much and to fear nothing as long
as I was in this world. I was not without money. I
gave her part of it and I paid the warder, out of what I
had left, a month's full board.

My money had a very good effect. I was put into
a decently furnished room and assured that Manon
had one like it. I immediately busied my mind with
ways to hasten my freedom. It was clear that there
was nothing absolutely criminal in my conduct; and
even supposing that the plan of our theft was proved
by Marcel's deposition, I knew very well that mere

intentions are not punishable. I resolved to write
promptly to my father and ask him to come to Paris
in person. I was much less ashamed, as I have already said, to be in the Châtelet than in Saint-Lazare.
Besides, although I preserved all the respect due to
the paternal authority, age and experience had greatly lessened my timidity. So I wrote, and they made
no difficulty at the Châtelet over allowing my letter to
go out. But this was a trouble I could have spared
myself if I had known that my father was to arrive
in Paris the next day.

He had received the letter I had written him a
week before. It had caused him extreme joy; but
however flattering the hope I had given him on the
subject of my conversion, he had not thought he
should rely completely on my promises. He had decided to come and assure himself of my change with
his own eyes, and to regulate his conduct according
to the sincerity of my repentance. He arrived the
day after my imprisonment. His first visit was the one
he paid Tiberge, to whom I had asked him to address his reply. He could not learn from him either
my address or my present condition. He found out
merely my principal adventures since I had escaped
from Saint-Sulpice. Tiberge spoke to him most ad-
vantageously about the inclinations toward goodness
that I had shown him in our last interview. He added
that he believed I was entirely free of Manon but
that he was nevertheless surprised that I had not
given him any news for a week. My father was no
dupe. He understood that there was something that
escaped Tiberge's penetration in the silence he complained of, and he went to such pains to pick up my
traces that two days after his arrival he learned I
was in the Châtelet.

Before receiving his visit, which I was far from
expecting so soon, I received that of the Lieutenant
General of Police; or, to call things by their names,
I underwent an interrogation. He offered me a few
reproaches, but they were neither harsh nor disagree-

able. He told me gently that he pitied my bad conduct;
that I had been unwise to make myself an enemy such
as Monsieur de G . . . M . . . ; that in truth it was easy
to note that there had been more imprudence and folly
in my case than malice; but that nevertheless this was
the second time I found myself subject to his jurisdic-
tion, and he had hoped I had become wiser after taking
two or three months of lessons at Saint-Lazare. Delighted to be dealing with a reasonable judge, I explained
myself to him in so respectful and moderate a manner
that he seemed extremely satisfied with my answers. He
told me that I should not give myself up too much to de-
spondency and that he felt disposed to do what he could
for me on account of my birth and my youth. I ven-
tured to commend Manon to him and praise her gentleness and natural goodness. He answered, laughing,
that he had not seen her yet, but that she was represented as a dangerous person. These words so ex-
cited my love that I told him a thousand passionate
things in defense of my poor mistress; and I could
not even help shedding a few tears. He ordered me
to be taken back to my room.

"Ah, love, love," exclaimed this grave magistrate
as he watched me leave, "will you never be reconciled with wisdom?"

I was turning over my ideas sadly and reflecting on
the conversation I had had with the Lieutenant General of Police when I heard the door to my room
open: it was my father. Although I ought to have
been half prepared for the sight of him, since I was
expecting it a few days later, I was nevertheless so
hard hit by it that I would have plunged into the
depths of the earth if it had opened at my feet. I went
and embraced him with every sign of extreme confusion. He sat down without either of us having yet
opened our mouth.

As I remained standing, with eyes downcast and
head uncovered,

"Sit down, sir," he said to me gravely, "sit down."
Thanks to the scandal of your debauchery and swindles,

I have discovered the place of your abode. It is the advantage of a merit such as yours that it cannot remain hidden. You are heading for renown by an infallible road. I trust that it will soon end at the Grêve[8] and that you will in fact have the glory of being exposed there to the wonder of all."

I made no answer. He went on:

"How unhappy a father is when, after loving a son tenderly and sparing nothing to make him a decent man, he finally finds only a knave who dishonors him! There is consolation for a reverse of fortune: time erases it, and the grief lessens; but what remedy is there for an evil that grows every day, such as the excesses of a vicious son who has lost all sense of honor? You aren't saying anything, you wretch," he added; "look at that counterfeit modesty and that hypocritical air of mildness; wouldn't anyone take him for the most honorable man of his family?"

Although I was obliged to recognize that I deserved a part of these insults, it seemed to me nevertheless that this was carrying them to excess. I thought it was permissible for me to explain naturally what was in my mind.

"I assure you, sir," I said to him, "that the modesty you see in me as I stand before you is not at all affected: it is the natural attitude of a wellborn son who has infinite respect for his father, especially an irritated father. Nor do I claim to pass as the most disciplined man in our family. I know I deserve your reproaches; but I entreat you to put a little more kindness into them and not treat me as the most infamous of all men. I do not merit such hard names. It is love, you know it, that has caused all my errors. Fatal passion! Alas! Don't you know its power, and can it be that your blood, which is the source of mine, has never felt the same fires? Love has made me too tender, too passionate, too faithful, and perhaps too indulgent toward the wishes of a wholly

---

[8] The Place de Grêve (now Place de l'Hôtel de Ville) was the site of the pillory and of public executions.

charming mistress: these are my crimes. Do you see one of them that dishonors you? Come, my dear father," I added tenderly, "have a little pity for a son who has always been full of respect and affection for you, who has not renounced honor and duty, as you think, and who is a thousand times more to be pitied than you can possibly imagine."

I shed a few tears as I finished these words.

A father's heart is the masterpiece of nature. She reigns in it, so to say, with indulgence, and she herself regulates all its movements. My father, who besides being a father was a man of intelligence and taste, was so touched by the turn I had given to my excuses that he had not the power to conceal his change of heart from me.

"Come, my poor Chevalier," he said to me, "come and embrace me; I do pity you."

I embraced him. He clasped me in a manner that made me judge what was going on in his heart.

"But then what means shall we adopt," he went on, "to get you out of here? Explain your whole story to me without disguise."

Since after all there was nothing in the main lines of my conduct that could absolutely dishonor me—at least gauging it by that of young men of a certain social rank—and since a mistress[9] does not pass for an infamy in this day and age, any more than a little skill in attracting good fortune in gambling, I gave my father sincerely the details of the life I had led. To each transgression that I admitted to him I took care to join famous examples, to minimize the shame.

"I am living with a mistress," I said to him, "without being bound by the marriage ceremonies: the duke of . . . keeps two in the eyes of all Paris; Monsieur de . . . [10] has had one for ten years whom he loves with a fidelity he never had for his wife; two-thirds of the gentlemen in France feel honored to have one. I have practiced some deceit in gambling;

9 1731 ed.: "a kept mistress."
10 1731 ed.: "Monsieur de F . . . ."

the marquis of . . . and the count of . . . have no other
source of revenue; the prince of . . . and the duke of
. . . are the leaders of a band of knights of the same
order."

As regards my designs on the purses of the two
G . . . M . . . 's, I could have proved just as easily that
I was not without models; but I had too much hon-
or left not to condemn myself together with all those
whose example I could have set myself; so that I
begged my father to forgive, for this weakness, the
two violent passions that had agitated me, vengeance
and love. He asked me whether I could give him any
insights into the quickest means of obtaining my freedom in a way that would allow him to avoid a sensation. I told him of the kindly feelings that the Lieutenant
General of Police had for me.

"If you find any difficulties," I said to him, "they
can come only from the G . . . M . . . 's; thus I think
it would be advisable for you to take the trouble to
see them."

He promised to do so. I did not dare ask him to
solicit for Manon. This was not a lack of boldness, but
an effect of the fear I had of outraging him by this
proposal and engendering in him some design fatal to
her and to me. I have yet to learn whether this fear
did not cause my greatest misfortunes, by keeping me
from testing out my father's dispositions and from
making an effort to inspire him with some favorable
to my unhappy mistress. Perhaps I might have
aroused his pity once more. I would have put him
on his guard against the impressions that he was
about to receive too readily from old G . . . M . . . .
Who knows? Perhaps my evil destiny would have won
out over all my efforts; but at least I would have
had only that and the cruelty of my enemies to
blame for my woe.

On leaving me, my father went and paid a visit to
Monsieur de G . . . M . . . . He found him with his
son, to whom the guardsman had honorably restored
his freedom. I never learned the particulars of their

conversation; but it has been only too easy to judge these by its fatal effects.

They went together—I mean the two fathers—and called on the Lieutenant General of Police, of whom they asked two favors: one, to let me out of the Châtelet at once; the other, to lock up Manon for the rest of her days or send her to America. At that time they were beginning to embark a large number of vagrants for the Mississippi. The Lieutenant General of Police gave them his word to have Manon leave on the first boat.

Monsieur de G . . . M . . . and my father together came immediately and brought me the news of my freedom. Monsieur de G . . . M . . . paid me a civil compliment on the past; and, having congratulated me on my good fortune in having such a father, he exhorted me henceforth to profit by his lessons and examples. My father ordered me to make my excuses to G . . . M . . . for the supposed injury I had done to his family and to thank him for having worked with him for my release. We went out together without having said a word about my mistress. I did not even dare speak about her to the turnkeys in their presence. Alas! My sad recommendations would have been quite useless. The cruel order had come at the same time as the one for my deliverance. That unfortunate girl was taken to the Hôpital one hour later to be put in with some wretched women who were condemned to undergo the same fate.

Since my father had obliged me to follow him to the house where he had taken lodgings, it was almost six in the evening when I found a moment to slip out of his sight and go back to the Châtelet. I was planning only to get some refreshments to Manon and commend her to the warder; for I had no confidence that I would be granted freedom to see her. I had not yet had time, either, to reflect on ways to deliver her.

I asked to speak to the warder. He had been pleased with my liberality and mildness; so that having some inclination to treat me kindly, he spoke to me of Manon's fate as a misfortune that he much regretted, because it might distress me. I did not comprehend this language at all. We talked for a few moments without understanding each other. Finally, perceiving that I needed an explanation, he gave it to me just as I have already had the horror to relate it to you, and as I still have, to repeat it.

Never had violent apoplexy a more sudden and terrible effect. I fell with so painful a palpitation of the heart that at the moment I lost consciousness I thought I was delivered from life forever. I even had something of this thought left when I came back to myself. I turned my eyes toward every part of the room and on myself to make certain whether I still had the unhappy attributes of a living man. It is certain that, if I had followed only the natural impulse which makes a being seek to deliver itself from its pains, nothing could have seemed to me sweeter than death, in that moment of despair and consternation. Religion itself could not make me picture anything more unbearable after death than the cruel convulsions that tortured me. However, by a miracle appropriate to love, I soon regained enough strength to thank Heaven for having restored my consciousness and reason. My death would have been useful only to me. Manon needed my life to deliver her, help her, avenge her. I swore to use myself unsparingly for this.

The warder gave me all the help I could have expected from the best of my friends. I accepted his services with keen gratitude.

"Alas!" I said to him. "So you are touched by my woes? Everyone abandons me. Even my father is doubtless one of my cruelest persecutors. No one has pity on me. You alone, in the abode of harshness and barbarity, you show compassion for the most miserable of all men!"

He advised me not to appear in the street without having recovered a little from being so upset.

"Let be, let be," I answered as I went out; "I shall see you again sooner than you think. Get the darkest of your dungeons ready for me; I shall work to deserve it."

Indeed my first resolutions came to nothing less than to do away with the two G . . . M . . . 's and the Lieutenant General of Police and then descend arms in hand on the Hôpital with everyone I could enlist in my quarrel. My father himself would hardly have been respected, in a vengeance that seemed to me so just; for the warder had not concealed from me that he and G . . . M . . . were the authors of my ruin.

But when I had taken a few steps in the streets and the air had cooled off my blood and my humors a bit, my frenzy gave way little by little to more reasonable feelings. The death of our enemies would have had scant usefulness for Manon, and would undoubtedly have exposed me to being deprived of all means of rescuing her. Besides, would I have had recourse to a cowardly murder? What other pathway could I open up for my vengeance? I collected all my powers and wits to work first for Manon's deliverance, putting off everything else until after the success of this important undertaking.

I had little money left. This was nevertheless a necessary base, with which I had to begin. I could see only three persons from whom I could expect any: Monsieur de T . . . , my father, and Tiberge. There was little likelihood of getting anything from the last two, and I was ashamed to weary the other by my importunities. But it is not in despair that you can observe the amenities. I went at once to the Seminary of Saint-Sulpice without worrying whether I should be recognized there. I asked for Tiberge. His first words let me understand that he still knew nothing of my latest adventures. This made me change the plan I had of trying to touch him with compassion. I told him in general of the pleasure I had had in seeing my father again, and I then asked him to lend me some money on the pretext of paying, before I left Paris, some debts that I wanted to keep unknown. He immediately gave me his purse. I took five hundred francs out of six hundred that I found in it. I offered him my note; he was too generous to accept it.

I turned from there to Monsieur de T . . . 's. I had no reserve with him. I exposed to him my misfortunes and my troubles; he already knew even the minutest details of these through the care he had taken to follow the adventure of young G . . . M. . . . He listened to me nevertheless and showed me much sympathy. When I asked him his advice on ways of delivering Manon, he answered sadly that he saw so small a ray that without some extraordinary help from Heaven I should give up hope; that he had gone specially to the Hôpital since she had been locked up there; that he himself had not been able to obtain permission to see her; that the orders of the Lieutenant General of Police were of the utmost rigor, and that as a crowning misfortune, the unhappy band which she was to join was destined to leave two days from now.

I was so taken aback by his remarks that he could have talked for an hour without my thinking of interrupting him. He went on to tell me that he had not gone to see me at the Châtelet in order to give himself more chance to serve me when he would be thought to have no link with me; that for the few hours I had been out of there he had been chagrined not to know where I had withdrawn to, and had wished to see me promptly to give me the only piece of advice that seemed possibly to offer hope for a change in Manon's lot—but dangerous advice, his part in which he begged me to conceal eternally: this was to choose a few bravoes who would have the courage to attack Manon's guards when they had left Paris with her. He did not wait for me to speak to him of my indigence.

"Here are a hundred pistoles," he said to me, presenting me with a purse, "which may be of some use to you. You will return them to me when fortune has set your affairs right again."

He added that if the concern for his reputation had allowed him to undertake the deliverance of my mistress himself, he would have offered me his arm and his sword.

This extreme generosity moved me to tears. To show him my gratitude I employed all the enthusiasm that my distress left me. I asked him if there was nothing to be hoped for from a series of intercessions with the Lieutenant General of Police. He told me that he had thought of it, but that he believed this was a useless resource because a pardon of that nature could not be requested without grounds, and he did not very well see what grounds one could use to get oneself a serious, powerful person as intercessor; that if one could have any hopes in that direction it could be only by making Monsieur de G . . . M . . . and my father change their feelings and prevailing on them to ask the Lieutenant General of Police themselves to revoke her sentence. He offered to make every effort to win over young G . . . M . . . , although he thought him a bit cooled in his regard by certain suspicions he had conceived about him on the occasion of our affair; and he exhorted me to omit nothing, for my part, to try to win over my father's mind.

This was no light undertaking for me; I say this not only because of the difficulty I must naturally find in overcoming his views, but for another reason which made me fear even to approach him: I had stolen away from his lodgings against his orders, and I had been firmly resolved not to return there ever since I had learned of Manon's sad destiny. I apprehended, with reason, that he might have me detained and taken back to the country in spite of myself. My elder brother had used this method before. It is true that I had grown older; but age was a feeble argument against force.

However, I found a way that saved me from that

danger: this was to get him to come to some public place and announce myself to him under another name. I immediately adopted this plan. Monsieur de T . . . went off to G . . . M . . .'s, and I to the Luxembourg, where I sent word to my father that a gentleman of his following was waiting to see him. I was afraid he might have some trouble in coming, because night was approaching. Nevertheless, he appeared soon after, followed by his lackey. I asked him to walk with me along a path where we could be alone. We went a hundred paces at least without speaking. No doubt he could well imagine that so many preparations had not been made without a purpose of some importance. He was waiting for my speech and I was meditating on it.

At last I opened my mouth.

"Sir," I said to him, trembling, "you are a good father. You have loaded me with favors and you have forgiven me an infinite number of faults. Accordingly Heaven is my witness that all my feelings for you are those of the most tender and respectful of sons. But it does seem to me . . . that your rigor . . ."

"Well? My rigor?" My father interrupted, no doubt finding that I was speaking too slowly for his impatience.

"Ah! sir," I went on, "it does seem to me that your rigor is extreme in the treatment you have given to the unfortunate Manon. You took Monsieur de G . . . M . . .'s word about her. His hatred represented her to you in the blackest colors. You formed a frightful idea of her. Yet she is the sweetest and most lovable creature that ever was. Why did it not please Heaven to make you want to see her for a moment! I am no surer that she is charming than I am that she would have seemed so to you. You would have taken her side. You would have loathed G . . . M . . .'s black artifices. You would have had compassion on her and on me. Alas! I am sure of it. Your heart is not insensible. You would have let yourself be touched."

He interrupted me again, seeing that I was speaking with an ardor that would not have allowed me to finish very soon. He wanted to know what I was intending to get at by such a passionate speech.

"At asking you for my life," I answered, "which I cannot retain for a moment if Manon once leaves for America."

"No, no," he said to me in a severe tone, "I would rather see you without life than without wisdom and honor."

"Then let us go no further!" I cried, taking him by the arm. "Take away this odious and unendurable life; for in the despair into which you are casting me, death will be a favor for me. It is a present worthy of a father's hand."

"I would be giving you only what you deserve," he replied. "I know many a father who would not have waited so long to make himself your executioner; but it is my excessive kindness that has ruined you."

I threw myself at his knees.

"Ah! If you have any of it left," I said, clasping them, "do not harden yourself against my tears. Think: I am your son. Alas! Remember my mother. You loved her so tenderly! Would you have suffered her to be torn from your arms? You would have defended her to the death. Do not others have a heart like yours? Can anyone be barbarously cruel after having once experienced what love and sorrow are?"

"Say no more to me about your mother," he retorted in an irritated voice; "that memory inflames my indignation. Your excesses would make her die of grief if she had lived long enough to see them. Let us end this talk," he added; "it distresses me, and will not make me change my resolve. I am going back to the house; I order you to follow me."

The dry hard tone with which he issued this order made me understand only too well that his heart was inflexible. I moved a few steps away for fear he might take a notion to detain me with his own hands.

"Do not increase my despair," I said to him, "by

forcing me to disobey you. It is impossible for me to follow you. It is no less so for me to live after the harshness with which you are treating me. Thus I bid you an eternal farewell. My death, of which you will soon learn," I added sadly, "will perhaps make you resume a father's feelings for me."

As I was turning away to leave him, he cried in violent anger:

"So you refuse to follow me? Go, run to your ruin. Farewell, ungrateful and rebellious son."

"Farewell!" I said to him in a transport of fury. "Farewell, barbarous and unnatural father."

I left the Luxembourg immediately. I walked through the streets like a madman as far as Monsieur de T . . .'s house. As I walked I raised my eyes and my hands to invoke the celestial powers.

"O Heaven!" I said. "Will you be as pitiless as men? I have no help left to look for unless from you."

Monsieur de T . . . had not yet returned home; but he came back after I had waited there a few moments for him. His negotiation had succeeded no better than mine. He told me so with a dejected face. Young G . . . M . . . , although less irritated than his father against Manon and me, had not been willing to undertake to plead with him in our favor. He had excused himself because of the fear he himself had of that vindictive old man, who had already gotten very angry with him in reproaching him with his plans for a liaison with Manon.

So the only way I had left was violence, such as Monsieur de T . . . had outlined to me; to this I reduced all my hopes.

"They are very uncertain," I said to him; "but the most solid and consoling of them for me is that of at least perishing in the attempt."

I left him, asking him to help me by his good wishes, and I no longer thought of anything but enlisting some comrades to whom I might communicate one spark of my own courage and resolution.

The first who came to my mind was the same
guardsman I had employed to hold up G . . . M . . . .
I also had the intention of going and spending the
night in his room, not having had my mind free enough
during the afternoon to procure myself a lodging. I
found him alone. It was a joy to him to see me out
of the Châtelet. He affectionately offered me his
services. I explained to him those that he could do
me. He had good sense enough to perceive all the
difficulties; but he was high-minded enough to undertake to surmount them. We spent part of the night
discussing my plan. He spoke to me of the three
soldiers of the guards whom he had used on the last
occasion as three men of tested bravery. Monsieur de
T . . . had informed me exactly of the number of archers who were to escort Manon; there were only six.
Five bold and resolute men were enough to strike
terror in these wretches, who are incapable of defending themselves honorably when they can avoid the
peril of combat by cowardice. Since I did not lack
money, the guardsman advised me to spare nothing
to ensure the success of our attack.

"We need horses," he said to me, "and pistols, and
a blunderbuss for each man. I'll be responsible for
taking care of these preparations tomorrow. We will
also need three civilian suits for our soldiers, who
would not dare appear in an affair of this nature in
their regimental uniform."

I put into his hands the hundred pistoles I had
received from Monsieur de T. . . . They were used up
the next day to the last sou. The three soldiers passed
in review before me. I incited them with great promises; and to rid them of all mistrust I began by
making them a present of ten pistoles each.

The day of carrying out our plan having come, I
sent one of them early in the morning to the Hôpital
to ascertain with his own eyes the moment when the
archers were to leave with their prey. Although I
had taken this precaution only out of an excess of
worry and forethought, it turned out to have been

absolutely necessary. I had been relying on some false information I had been given about their route, and having persuaded myself that it was at La Rochelle that this pathetic troop was to be put on board, I would have wasted my pains waiting for them on the road to Orléans. However, I was informed by the report of the soldier in the guards that they were taking the road to Normandy and that it was from Le Havre that they were to set out for America.

We immediately went to the Porte Saint-Honoré, being careful to walk by different streets. We met at the end of the *faubourg*. Our horses were fresh. We were not long in spying the six guards and the two wretched wagons which you saw at Pacy two years ago. This spectacle almost deprived me of strength and consciousness.

"O fortune," I exclaimed, "cruel fortune! Here at least grant me death or victory."

We held council for a moment on the way we would make our attack. The archers were hardly more than four hundred paces ahead of us, and we could cut them off by crossing a little field around which the highroad wound. The guardsman was minded to take this course to surprise them by suddenly descending on them. I approved of his idea and was the first to spur my horse. But fortune had pitilessly rejected my prayers.

The archers, seeing five horsemen bearing down on them, had no doubt that it was to attack them. They took up a position of defense, readying their bayonets and guns with quite a resolute air. The sight of this, which only animated the guardsman and me, all of a sudden drained all courage out of our three cowardly companions. They stopped as if in concert, and, having said to one another a few words that I did not hear, turned their horses' heads about and regained the road for Paris full tilt.

"Ye Gods!" said the guardsman, who appeared as frantic as I at this infamous desertion. "What are we going to do? There are only two of us."

I had lost my voice from fury and astonishment. I stopped, uncertain whether my first vengeance should not be employed in the pursuit and chastisement of the cowards who were abandoning me. I was watching them flee, and casting my eyes in the other direction upon the archers. If it had been possible to divide myself in two, I would have fallen simultaneously upon these two objects of my rage; I would have devoured them all together. The guardsman, who could judge my uncertainty by the frantic movement of my eyes, begged me to listen to his advice.

"Being only two," he said to me, "we would be mad to attack six men as well armed as we are and who appear to be waiting for us and standing firm. We must go back to Paris and try to succeed better in the choice of our bravoes. The archers cannot possibly cover much ground each day with two heavy wagons; we will overtake them again tomorrow without any trouble."

I reflected a moment on this plan; but, seeing nothing on all sides save reasons for despair, I adopted a truly desperate resolution. This was to let my companion go with thanks for his services; and far from attacking the archers, I resolved to go and ask them submissively to receive me into their party, so as to accompany Manon, with them, to Le Havre, and then go overseas with her.

"Everyone persecutes me or betrays me," I said to the guardsman. "I cannot rely on anyone any more. I expect nothing more either from fortune or from human help. My woes are at their height; I have nothing left to do but submit to them. So I close my eyes to all hope. May Heaven reward your nobility! Farewell! I shall assist my evil destiny to consummate my ruin by voluntarily running to meet it myself."

He made vain efforts to persuade me to go back to Paris. I asked him to let me follow my resolution and to leave me at once, for fear the archers should continue to believe that our plan was to attack them.

I went toward them alone, at a slow pace, my face

so dismayed that they must have found nothing frightening in my approach. Nevertheless they kept their defensive position.

"Be assured, gentlemen," I said as I came up to them, "I do not bring war, I come to ask favors of you."

I asked them to continue on their way without mistrust, and I told them, as we went along, the favors I expected of them. They consulted together on the way they should receive this overture. The leader of the band spoke up for the others. He replied that their orders to watch over their captives were extremely rigorous; that nevertheless I seemed such a nice young man that he and his comrades would relax a little from their duty; but that I must understand this would have to cost me something. I had about fifteen pistoles left; I told them, naturally, what were the resources of my purse.

"Well," said the archer to me, "we will treat you generously. It will cost you only one crown per hour to converse with whichever of our wenches you like best; that's the current Paris price."

I had not spoken to him about Manon in particular because I had no intention that they should know about my passion. They at first imagined it was only a young man's fancy that made me seek a little amusement with these creatures; but when they thought they had observed that I was in love, they raised the tribute I had to pay so much that my purse was exhausted by the time we left Mantes, where we had spent the night before we reached Pacy.

Shall I tell you what was the pitiful subject of my talks with Manon during this journey, or what impression the sight of her made on me when I had obtained leave from the guards to approach her cart? Ah! Words never can render more than half the feelings of the heart; but picture my poor mistress chained around the waist, sitting on a few handfuls of straw, her head leaning listlessly on one side of the wagon, her face pale and wet with a stream of tears that forced their way out between her eyelids, although she kept her eyes continually shut. She had not even had the curiosity to open them on hearing the noise of her guards when they were afraid of being attacked. Her linen was dirty and disarranged, her delicate hands exposed to the ravages of the air; in short, this whole compound of loveliness, this face capable of bringing the universe back to idolatry, appeared in inexpressible disorder and dejection. I spent some time gazing at her, riding my horse along beside the cart. I was so far from self-possessed that I was several times on the point of taking a dangerous fall. My sighs and frequent exclamations attracted a few glances from her. She recognized me, and I noted that on her first impulse she tried to throw herself out of the wagon to come to me; but, being held back by her chain, she fell back into her former attitude.

I begged the archers to stop a moment out of compassion; they consented out of avarice. I got off my horse and sat down beside her. She was so languid and weakened that she was a long time without being able to use her tongue or move her hands. Meanwhile I bathed them with my tears; and since I was unable to utter a single word myself, we were both in one of the saddest situations ever known. Our words were no less so when we recovered our ability to speak.

Manon spoke little; it seemed that shame and grief had altered her organs of speech; her voice sounded weak and trembling. She thanked me for not forgetting her and for giving her the satisfaction, she said with a sigh, of seeing me at least one more time and bidding me a final farewell. But when I assured her that nothing was capable of separating me from her and that I intended to follow her to the end of the world to take care of her, to serve her, to love her, and to attach my miserable destiny inseparably to hers, the poor girl gave herself up to such tender and sorrowful feelings that I had some fear for her life from such a violent emotion. Every movement of her soul seemed to gather in her eyes. She kept them

fixed on me. Sometimes she opened her mouth without having the strength to finish the few words that
she began. Some of these escaped her nevertheless.
They were marks of wonder at my love, tender notes
of pity at its excess, doubts that she could be fortunate enough to have inspired so perfect a passion in
me, pleas to make me give up the plan of following her
and seek elsewhere a happiness worthy of me, which
she told me I could not hope for with her.

In spite of the cruelest of all fates, I found my
felicity in her glances and in the certainty I had of
her affection. True, I had lost all that other men esteem; but I was master of Manon's heart, the only
good that I esteemed. In Europe, in America, what
did it matter to me where I lived, if I was sure to
be happy living there with my mistress? Isn't the
whole universe a homeland for two faithful lovers?
Don't they find in one another father, mother, relatives, friends, riches, and happiness? If anything caused
me anxiety, it was the fear of seeing Manon exposed
to the privations of indigence. I already imagined
myself with her in some wild region inhabited by savages.

"I am very sure," I said to myself, "that there
could not be any as cruel as G ... M ... and my
father. They will at least let us live in peace. If the
accounts we are given of them are faithful, they
follow the laws of nature. They know neither the
frenzies of avarice that possess G ... M ..., nor the
fantastic notions of honor that have made my father
my enemy. They will not trouble two lovers whom they
see living as simply as they do."

So I was tranquil on that score. But I did not form
any romantic notions in regard to the ordinary needs
of life. I had experienced all too often that there are
unbearable privations, especially for a delicate girl
who is accustomed to a comfortable and abundant
life. I was in despair at having vainly exhausted my
purse, and that the little money I had left was also
on the point of being filched from me by the knav-

ery of the archers. I supposed that with a small sum
I might have hoped, not only to hold out for some
time against misery in America, where money was
scarce, but even to make some plan there for a last-
ing situation. This consideration made me think of
writing to Tiberge, whom I had always found so
prompt to offer me the help of friendship. At the
first town we passed, I wrote. I offered him no other
motive than the pressing need I foresaw I should be
in at Le Havre, where I confessed to him I had
gone to accompany Manon. I asked him for a hundred pistoles.

"Send them to me at Le Havre," I told him, "by
the postmaster. You can well see that this is the last
time I will impose on your affection, and that since
my unhappy mistress is being taken from me forever,
I cannot let her leave without some alleviations to
mitigate her lot and my mortal regrets."

The archers became so intractable, when they had
discovered the violence of my passion, that, continually
redoubling the price of their slightest favors, they soon
reduced me to the utmost poverty. Besides, love hardly
allowed me to spare my purse. I forgot myself from
morning to evening beside Manon, and it was no longer
by the hour that time was measured out to me; it
was by the length of whole days. Finally, my purse
being completely empty, I found myself exposed to
the caprices and brutality of six wretches, who treated
me with intolerable insolence. You were witness to
this at Pacy. Meeting you was a happy moment of
respite which was granted me by fortune. Your pity
at the sight of my sorrows was my only recommendation to your generous heart. The help that you liberally granted me enabled me to reach Le Havre,
and the archers kept their promise with more fidelity
than I had hoped.

We arrived at Le Havre. I first went to the post
office. Tiberge had not yet had time to answer me. I inquired on exactly what day I might expect his letter.
It could not arrive until two days later; and by a

strange arrangement of my evil lot, it happened that our vessel was to leave on the morning of the day when I was expecting the post. I cannot describe to you my despair.

"What!" I cried. "Even in misfortune I must always be singled out for extremes!"

Manon replied:

"Alas! Does a life so unhappy deserve the care we take over it? Let us die at Le Havre, my dear Chevalier. Let death put a sudden end to our miseries! Shall we go and drag them to an unknown land, where no doubt we must expect the extremes of horror, since they decided to make it a punishment for me? Let us die," she repeated, "or at least give me death, and go and seek another lot in the arms of a more fortunate mistress."

"No, no," I told her, "for me it is an enviable lot to be unhappy with you."

Her words made me tremble. I judged that she was overwhelmed by her woes. I tried to assume a more tranquil air to rid her of these dire thoughts of death and despair. I resolved to maintain the same conduct in the future; and since that time experience has shown me that nothing is more capable of inspiring courage in a woman than the fearlessness of a man she loves.

When I had lost hope of receiving help from Tiberge, I sold my horse. The money I derived from this, added to what I still had left from your liberalities, amounted to the small sum of seventeen pistoles. I used seven of them for the purchase of a few comforts necessary for Manon; and I put away the other ten carefully as the foundation of our fortune and of our hopes in America. I had no trouble in having myself received on the ship. They were looking then for young men who were disposed to join the colony voluntarily. Passage and food were accorded me gratis. Since the mail for Paris was to go out the next day, I left in it a letter for Tiberge. It was touching, and no doubt capable of moving him to the utmost, since it made him form a resolve which could come only from an infinite depth of tenderness and generosity for an unhappy friend.

We set sail. The wind never failed to be favorable. I obtained from the captain a room apart for Manon and me. He had the kindness to look upon us with another eye than on the common lot of our miserable associates. I had taken him aside privately on the first day and, to attract from him some personal consideration, I had revealed to him a part of my misfortunes. I did not think myself guilty of a shameful lie in telling him that I was married to Manon. He pretended to believe it and granted me his protection. We received marks of this during the whole navigation. He took care to have us decently fed; and the consideration he showed us served to make us respected by our companions in misery. I was continually attentive so as not to let Manon suffer the slightest discomfort. She was well aware of this; and the sight of it, combined with the keen sense of the strange extremity to which I had reduced myself for her, made her so tender and passionate, so attentive herself to my slightest needs, that between her and me it was a perpetual emulation in service and in love. I had no regrets for Europe. On the contrary, the further we advanced toward America, the more I felt my heart expand and grow tranquil. If I could have been sure of not lacking the absolute necessities of life there, I would have thanked fortune for having given so favorable a turn to our woes.

After two months of navigation we at last approached the desired shores. The country offered us nothing pleasant at first sight. It consisted of sterile and uninhabited plains in which you saw scarcely a few reeds and a few trees stripped bare by the wind. No trace of men or animals. However, the captain having fired a few pieces of our artillery, we were not long in perceiving a group of citizens of the new

Orléans[11] who approached us with lively signs of
joy. We had not made out the town. It is hidden
from that direction by a little hill. We were received
like people descended from Heaven.

These poor inhabitants pressed to ask us a thousand questions about the state of France and the different provinces in which they were born. They
embraced us as their own brothers and as dear comrades who had come to share their misery and lone-
liness. We set out on the road to town with them,
but we were surprised to discover as we went along
that what had up till then been vaunted to us as a
fine town was only a collection of a few wretched
shacks. These were inhabited by five or six hundred
persons. The governor's house seemed to us distinguished a bit by its height and its situation. It is
defended by a few earthworks, around which extends
a wide moat.

First we were introduced to him. He had a long
talk with the captain in private, and then, coming
back to us, he looked over, one after the other, all
the girls who had arrived on the ship. They were
thirty in number, for at Le Havre we had found
another band of which had joined ours. The
governor, having examined them at length, sent for
various young men of the town who had been waiting and pining for a wife. To the principal ones he
gave the prettiest girls, and lots were drawn for the
rest. He had not yet spoken to Manon; but when he
had ordered the others to withdraw, he had us both
stay.

"I am told by the captain," he said to us, "that
you are married, and that on the voyage he has recognized you as two persons of intelligence and merit.
I am not going into the reasons that have caused
your misfortune; but if it is true that you have as
much breeding as your appearance promises, I shall
spare no pains to alleviate your lot, and you your-

[11] Prévost consistently uses this form, which was normal in
his time. Hereafter it will be translated as New Orleans.

selves will contribute to make me find more attraction in this wild and desolate place."

I answered him in the manner I thought most appropriate to confirm the idea he had of us. He gave a few orders, to have a lodging prepared for us in the town, and kept us for supper with him. I found him very polite for a governor of wretched exiles. He asked us no questions in public about the details of our adventures. The conversation was general; and in spite of our sadness, Manon and I made an effort to make it agreeable.

In the evening he had us escorted to the lodging that had been prepared for us. We found a miserable shack, composed of planks and mud, which consisted of two or three rooms[12] on the ground floor with an attic above. He had had five or six chairs put in, and a few commodities necessary for life. Manon appeared frightened at the sight of so sad an abode. It was for me that she was distressed, much more than for herself. She sat down, when we were alone, and began weeping bitterly. I tried at first to console her. But when she made me understand that it was I alone she was sorry for, and that in our common woes she was considering only what I had to suffer, I put on a show of enough courage, and even enough joy, to inspire some in her.

"What should I complain of?" I said to her. "I possess everything I desire. You love me, don't you? What other happiness have I ever aspired to? Let us leave to Heaven the care of our destiny. I do not find it so desperate. The governor is a civil man; he has shown us consideration; he will not allow us to lack necessities. As regards the poverty of our shack and the coarseness of our furniture, you may have noticed that there are few persons here who appear better lodged and furnished than we are; and besides," I added, kissing her, "you are a wonderful alchemist; you transform everything into gold."

[12] 1731 ed.: "two rooms." Again below: "two or three chairs."

"Then you will be the richest person in the universe," she answered; "for if there was never a love such as yours, it is also impossible to be loved more tenderly than you are. I judge myself," she went on. "I clearly feel that I have never deserved this prodigious attachment that you have for me. I have caused you pains for which you could not forgive me except for your extreme goodness. I have been frivolous and fickle; and even while loving you to distraction, as I have always done, I was nothing but an ingrate. But you cannot believe how much I have changed. My tears, which you have seen flow so often since we left France, have never once had my woes as their cause. I ceased to feel these as soon as you began to share them. I have wept only out of tenderness and compassion for you. I cannot console myself for having been able to hurt you for a single moment in my life. I never cease to reproach myself for my inconstancies, and to be touched as I marvel at what love has made you capable of doing for a wretched woman who was not worthy of it—and who," she added with a flood of tears, "could never pay even with all her blood for half the sorrows she has caused you."

Her tears, her words, and the tone in which she uttered them, made such an astounding impression on me that I seemed to feel my whole soul split in two.

"Be careful," I said, "be careful, my dear Manon. I haven't the strength to bear such keen signs of your affection; I am not accustomed to these excesses of joy. O God!" I cried, "I ask nothing more of You. I am assured of Manon's heart; it is just as I have desired it to make me happy; I can no longer cease to be so now. My felicity is well established."

"It is," she replied, "if you make it depend on me, and I know well where I too can count on always finding mine."

I went to bed with these charming ideas in mind, which changed my hut into a palace worthy of the greatest king in the world. After this, America appeared to me a place of delight.

"It is to New Orleans that people must come," I often said to Manon, "when they want to taste the true sweets of love. It is here that they love each other without self-interest, without jealousy, without inconstancy. Our compatriots come here to seek gold; they never imagine that we have found here far more precious treasures."

We carefully cultivated the governor's friendship. He had the kindness, a few weeks after our arrival, to give me a small post that came to be vacant in the fort. Although it was not very distinguished, I accepted it as a favor from Heaven. It put me in a position to live without being a burden to anyone. I took a valet for myself and a maid for Manon. Our little fortune became settled. I was regular in my conduct. Manon was no less so. We let no opportunity escape us to be serviceable and do good to our neighbors. This obliging disposition and the sweetness of our manners won us the trust and affection of the whole colony. In a short time we were so well thought of that we were considered the first persons of the town after the governor.

The innocence of our occupations and the tranquillity in which we continually lived served imperceptibly to recall to us thoughts of religion. Manon had never been an impious girl. Neither was I one of those extreme freethinkers who glory in adding irreligion to moral depravity. Love and youth had caused all our excesses. Experience was beginning to take the place of age for us; it had the same effect on us as years. Our conversations, which were always thoughtful, brought us imperceptibly to a desire for a virtuous love. I was the first to propose this change to Manon. I knew the principles of her heart, She was straight and natural in all her feelings, a quality which always inclines a person to virtue. I made her understand that there was one thing lacking to our happiness.

"That," I said to her, "is to have the approval of Heaven. We have souls too fair, and hearts too sound, both of us, to live willingly forgetful of duty. Enough to have lived so in France, where it was equally impossible to stop loving each other and to satisfy ourselves in a legitimate way; but in America, where we depend only on ourselves, where we no longer have to reckon with the arbitrary laws of rank and convention, where we are even thought to be married, what keeps us from being so in fact and ennobling our love by the vows that religion authorizes? As for me," I added, "I offer you nothing new in offering you my heart and my hand; but I am ready to renew the gift of them to you at the foot of an altar."

It seemed to me that this speech pierced her with joy.

"Would you believe," she replied, "that I have thought of that a thousand times since we have been in America? Fear of displeasing you made me lock up this wish in my heart. I do not have the presumption of aspiring to the rank of being your wife."

"Ah! Manon," I replied, "you would soon be wife to a king, if Heaven had had me born to a crown. Let us hesitate no longer. We have no obstacle to fear. I mean to speak about this today to the governor and admit to him that we have deceived him up to this day. Let us leave it to vulgar lovers," I added, "to fear the indissoluble chains of marriage. They would not fear them if, like us, they were sure of bearing always those of love."

I left Manon overwhelmed with joy after this resolve.

I am persuaded that there is not an honorable man in the world who would not have approved my views in the circumstances I was in, that is, fatally enslaved to a passion that I could not conquer and attacked by remorse which I must not stifle. But will there be anyone who will accuse my complaints of injustice if I bemoan the rigor of Heaven in rejecting a plan I had formed only to propitiate it? Alas!

What am I saying, rejecting? Heaven punished it like a crime. It had suffered me with patience while I was walking blindly in the path of vice, and its harshest chastisements were reserved for me when I should begin to return to virtue. I fear I may lack strength to complete the story of the most disastrous event that ever was.

I went to the governor's as I had agreed with Manon, to ask him to consent to the ceremony of our marriage. I would have been careful not to speak about it to him or to anyone else, if I could have promised myself that his almoner, who was then the only priest in the town, would have done me this service without his participation; but, not daring to hope that he would pledge himself to silence, I had decided to act openly.

The governor had a nephew named Synnelet, who was extremely dear to him. He was a man of about thirty, brave, but headstrong and violent. He was not married. Manon's beauty had struck him from the day we arrived; and the numberless occasions he had had to see her in nine or ten months had so inflamed his passion that he was burning for her in secret. However, as he was convinced, like his uncle and indeed the whole town, that I was really married, he had made himself master of his love to the point of letting no spark of it appear, and he had even shown a zealous friendliness for me and done me a service on several occasions. I found him with his uncle when I arrived at the fort. I had no reason to oblige me to keep my intention a secret from him, so I made no difficulty about explaining myself in his presence. The governor listened to me with his usual kindness. I told him part of my story, which he heard with pleasure; and when I asked him to be present at the ceremony that I had in mind, he had the generosity to undertake to meet all the expenses of the festivities. I went away very satisfied.

An hour later I saw the almoner come into my house. I imagined that he was coming to give me a

few instructions about my wedding; but, after greet-
ing me coldly, he informed me in a word or two that
my lord the governor forbade me to think about it
and that he had other views for Manon.

"Other views for Manon!" I said to him with a
deadly clutching at my heart. "And what views, pray,
Sir Almoner?"

He answered that I was not unaware that my lord
the governor was the master; that since Manon had
been sent from France for the colony, it was up to
him to dispose of her; that he had not done so until
then, because he thought she was married; but that
having learned from my own lips that she was not,
he saw fit to give her to Monsieur Synnelet, who was
in love with her. My temper got the better of my
prudence. I haughtily ordered the almoner to leave
my house, swearing that the governor, Synnelet, and
the whole town together would not dare lay a hand
on my wife, or my mistress, whichever they chose
to call her.

I immediately imparted to Manon the dire message I had just received. We judged that Synnelet
had seduced his uncle's mind after I came back
home, and that this was the outcome of some long-
premeditated plan. They were the stronger. We were
situated in New Orleans as if in the middle of the
sea, that is to say separated by immense distances
from the rest of the world. Where could we flee, in
an unknown land, deserted, or inhabited by wild
beasts and by savages as inhuman as they? I was esteemed in the town, but I could not hope to rouse
the people in my favor enough to hope for help proportionate to my trouble. I would have needed
money; I was poor. Besides, the outcome of a popular uprising was uncertain, and if fortune had failed
us our plight would become irremediable.

I was turning over all these thoughts in my mind;
communicating part of them to Manon; forming new
ones without listening to her answer. I would make
one decision, reject it to make another. I was talking

to myself, answering my own thoughts out loud. In short, I was in a state of agitation which I cannot compare to anything, because there never was one to equal it. Manon had her eyes on me. She judged from my confusion the greatness of the peril; and trembling for me more than for herself, that tender girl dared not even open her mouth to express her fears to me.

After countless reflections, I settled on the resolution of going to see the governor to try to move him by considerations of honor and by the memory of my respect and his affection. Manon tried to oppose my leaving. She said to me with tears in her eyes:

"You are going to your death. They are going to kill you. I shall never see you again. I want to die before you."

It took considerable efforts to persuade her of the necessity of my leaving and of her staying in the house. I promised her that she would see me again in a moment. She was unaware, and so was I, that it was upon herself that all the wrath of Heaven and the fury of our enemies was to fall.

I went to the fort. The governor was with his almoner. I abased myself, in order to touch him, to the point of a submissiveness that would have made me die of shame if I had shown it in any other cause. I besieged him with every motive that is bound to make a sure impression on any heart which is not that of a cruel, ferocious tiger. That barbarian made only two replies to my complaints, and repeated them a hundred times: Manon, he told me, depended on him; he had given his word to his nephew.

I was resolved to control myself to the last. I contented myself with telling him I thought he was too much my friend to want my death, to which I would consent sooner than to the loss of my mistress.

I was only too well persuaded when I left that I had nothing to hope for from this obstinate old man, who would have damned himself a thousand times for his nephew. However, I persisted in my plan to maintain an air of moderation to the very end, resolved, if they went to extremes of injustice, to offer America one of the bloodiest and most horrible spectacles that love has ever produced. I was on my way back home, meditating on this plan, when fate, wanting to hasten my ruin, made me encounter Synnelet. He read in my eyes a part of my thoughts. I have said that he was brave; he came up to me.

"Aren't you looking for me?" he said. "I know that my intentions offend you, and I have clearly foreseen that you and I would have to cut each other's throats. Let's go see which will be the more fortunate."

I answered that he was right, and that there was nothing but my death that could end our differences. We went off about a hundred paces outside the town. Our swords crossed; I wounded him, and disarmed him almost at the same time. He was so enraged by this mishap that he refused to ask me for his life and to give up Manon. Perhaps I had the right to take both from him at one blow; but noble blood never belies itself. I threw him his sword.

"Let us begin again," I said to him, "and remember, no quarter."

He attacked me with unutterable fury. I must confess that I was not good with weapons, having had only three months' training in Paris. Love guided my sword. Synnelet did not fail to pierce my arm through and through; but I caught him on the return and dealt him such a vigorous thrust that he fell motionless at my feet.

In spite of the joy that victory gives after a mortal combat, I immediately reflected on the consequences of this death. There was for me no hope of mercy or delay of execution. Knowing as I did the governor's passion for his nephew, I was certain that my death would not be deferred for one hour after his was known. Pressing though that fear was, it was not the strongest cause of my anxiety. Manon, Manon's welfare, her peril, and the necessity of losing her, troubled me to the point of spreading darkness over my eyes and keeping me from recognizing the place I was in. I envied Synnelet's fate; a swift death seemed to me the only remedy for my woes. However, it was this very thought which made me sharply summon back my senses and rendered me capable of making a resolve.

"What! I want to die," I exclaimed, "to end my woes? Then there are some that I fear more than the loss of the one I love? Ah! Rather suffer even the cruelest extremities to help my mistress; and put off dying until I have suffered them in vain."

I took the road back to the town. I entered my house. There I found Manon half dead with fright and anxiety. My presence revived her. I could not disguise to her the terrible accident that had just happened to me. She fell into my arms unconscious at the story of Synnelet's death and my wound. I spent more than a quarter of an hour bringing her back to her senses.

I was half dead myself. I could not see the slightest gleam of hope for her safety or my own.

"Manon, what shall we do?" I said to her when she had recovered a little strength. "Alas! What are we to do? I absolutely must go away. Do you want to stay in the town? Yes, stay here. You may still be happy here; and I shall go, far from you, to seek death among savages or in the claws of wild beasts."

She rose in spite of her weakness. She took me by the hand and led me to the door.

"Let us flee together," she said; "let us not lose a moment. Synnelet's body may by chance have been found, and we might not have time to get away."

"But, dear Manon!" I replied in complete bewilderment, "then tell me where we can go. Do you see any resource? Isn't it better for you to try to live here without me, and for me to offer my head voluntarily to the governor?"

That proposal only increased her ardor to leave. I

had to follow her. I still had enough presence of mind, as I went out, to take a few strong liquors that I had in my room and all the provisions that I could get into my pockets. We told our servants, who were in the next room, that we were going out for our evening walk; this was our habit every day; and we went away from the town more rapidly than Manon's delicacy seemed to allow.

Although I had not come out of my irresolution about the place for us to withdraw to, I was not without two hopes, but for which I would have preferred death to the uncertainty about what might happen to Manon.

I had acquired enough knowledge of the country, in almost ten months that I had been in America, not to be unaware of the way one could have friendly dealings with the savages. It was possible to put oneself in their hands without running into certain death. I had even learned a few words of their language and a few of their customs on the various occasions I had had of seeing them.

Besides this pitiful resource, I had another in the persons of the English, who, like ourselves, have settlements in that part of the New World. But I was frightened at the distance. We had to cross, to reach their colonies, sterile countrysides many days' journey in width, and some mountains so high and steep that the way over seemed difficult even for the toughest and most vigorous men. I flattered myself nonetheless that we might take advantage of these two resources: the savages to help guide us, and the English to receive us into their habitations.

We walked as long as Manon's courage could sustain her, that is to say for about two leagues; for this incomparable mistress steadfastly refused to stop any sooner. Overwhelmed at last with fatigue, she confessed to me that it was impossible for her to go any further. It was already night. We sat down in the middle of a vast plain, having been unable to find a tree to give us shelter. Her first care was to change the bandage on my wound, which she herself had dressed before we left. In vain I opposed her wishes. I would have dealt her the last mortal blow if I had refused her the satisfaction of believing I was comfortable and out of danger before thinking of her own preservation. For a few moments I submitted to her wishes. I received her attentions in silence and with shame. But when she had satisfied her tenderness, with what ardor did not mine take its turn! I stripped myself of all my clothes and stretched them under her to make her find the ground less hard. I made her consent, in spite of herself, to let me do everything I could think of to make her less uncomfortable. I warmed her hands with my burning kisses and the heat of my sighs. I spent the whole night watching by her side and praying Heaven to grant her a sweet and peaceful sleep. O God! How fervent and sincere were my prayers! And by what a rigorous judgment had You resolved not to grant them!

Forgive me if I finish in a few words a story that kills me. I am telling you of a misfortune without precedent. My whole life is devoted to weeping over it. But although I bear it ever present in my memory, my soul seems to recoil in horror each time I try to tell of it.

We had spent part of the night tranquilly. I thought my dear mistress asleep, and I dared not even breathe for fear of disturbing her repose. By daybreak I noticed, on touching her hands, that they were cold and trembling. I drew them to my breast to warm them. She felt this movement; and, making an effort to seize mine, she told me in a weak voice that she thought her last hour had come. At first I took these words only for a language common in misfortune, and I answered them only with the tender consolations of love. But her frequent sighs, her silence at my questions, the clasp of her hands, in which she continued to hold mine, made me recognize that the end of her misfortunes was approaching. Do not ask me to describe my feelings or report her last words. I lost her; I received tokens of love from her even at the moment she was dying; that is all I have the strength to tell you of that fatal and deplorable event.

My soul did not follow hers. No doubt Heaven did not consider me punished rigorously enough. It willed that I should since drag out a listless and miserable life. I willingly renounce ever living a happier one.

I remained for more than twenty-four hours[13] with my lips pressed to the face and hands of my dear Manon. My intention was to die there, but at the beginning of the second day[14] I reflected that her body would be exposed after my decease to be the prey of wild beasts. I formed the resolution to bury her and to wait for death on her grave. I was already so near my end from the weakness caused me by fasting and grief that I needed many efforts to stand up. I was obliged to have recourse to the spirits I had brought. They gave me as much strength as I needed for the sad service I was to perform. It was not hard for me to open up the ground in the place where I was. It was a plain covered with sand. I broke my sword so as to use it to dig with; but I derived less help from it than from my hands. I opened up a wide pit. In it I placed the idol of my heart, after taking care to wrap her in all my clothes so as to keep the sand from touching her. I put her in that place only after kissing her a thousand times with all the ardor of the most perfect love. I sat down again near her. I gazed at her for a long time. I could not bring myself to close up her grave. Finally, as my strength again began to weaken, fearing it might fail me completely before I finished my task, I buried forever in the bosom of Earth the most perfect and lovely thing she ever bore. I then lay down upon the grave, my face turned to the sand; and closing my eyes with the intention of never open-

13 1731 ed.: "two days and two nights."
14 1731 ed.: "the third day."

ing them again, I invoked the aid of Heaven and
waited impatiently for death.

What will seem to you difficult to believe is that
all the time I was carrying out this lugubrious minis-
try not a tear came from my eyes nor a sigh from
my mouth. The profound consternation I was in,
and my determined intention to die, had cut off the
channels for every expression of despair and grief.
And so I did not remain long, in the posture I was
in upon the grave, without losing what little consciousness and feeling I had left.

After what you have just heard, the conclusion
of my story is of so little importance as not to be
worth the trouble you are good enough to take to
listen to it. When Synnelet's body was brought back
to the town and his wounds examined with care, it
turned out not only that he was not dead, but that
he had not even received any dangerous wound. He
informed his uncle of the way things had happened
between us, and his generosity impelled him to publish immediately the effects of mine. They sent to
look for me; and my absence with Manon made me
suspected of having decided on flight. It was too late
to send anyone on my tracks; but the next day and
the day after that were spent in pursuit of me. I
was found on Manon's grave with no sign of life,
and those who discovered me in that state, seeing
me almost naked and bleeding from my wound,
did not doubt that I had been robbed and murdered.
They carried me to the town. The movement of the
carrying revived my senses. The sighs I uttered, on
opening my eyes and groaning to find myself back
among the living, let them know that I was still in
condition to receive help. It was given and was all
too successful.

Nevertheless I was locked up in a tight prison.
The case against me was drawn up, and, since Manon did not appear, I was accused of having done
away with her in a fit of rage and jealousy. I related, naturally, my pitiful adventure. Synnelet, in

spite of the transports of sorrow into which this story cast him, had the generosity to solicit my pardon. He obtained it.

I was so weak that they were obliged to carry me from the prison into my bed, where I was kept for three months by a violent illness. My hatred for life did not diminish. I continually called on death and was long obstinate in rejecting all remedies. But Heaven, after having punished me with so much rigor, planned to make my sorrows, and its chastisements, useful to me. It shed upon me its light, which made me recall ideas worthy of my birth and my education.[15] Tranquility having begun to revive a little in my soul, this change was closely followed by my cure. I gave myself up entirely to the promptings of honor,[16] and I continued to fill my little position while waiting for the ships from France which go once each year to that part of America. I was resolved to return to my native land and there atone, by a wise and orderly life, for the scandal of my conduct. Synnelet had taken care to have my dear mistress' body transported to an honorable place.

It was about six weeks after my recovery that, walking alone one day along the shore, I saw a ship arrive which the business of trade brought to New Orleans. I attentively watched people disembark. I was struck with extreme surprise on recognizing Tiberge among those advancing toward the town. That faithful friend recognized me from far off, in spite of the changes that sadness had wrought in my face. He informed me that the sole motive of his voyage had been the desire to see me and prevail upon me to return to France; having received the letter I had written him from Le Havre, he had gone there in person to bring me the help I was asking for; he had felt the keenest sorrow on learning of my departure

---

15 1731 ed.: "It shed upon me the light of its grace, and inspired in me the plan to return to it by the paths of penitence."

16 1731 ed.: "to the practice of piety."

and would have left at once, to follow me, if he had found a ship ready to set sail; he had looked for one for several months in various ports and, having finally come upon one in Saint-Malo about to weigh anchor for Martinique, he had embarked in the hope of procuring an easy passage from there to New Orleans; the Saint-Malo vessel having been captured on the way by Spanish corsairs and taken to one of their islands, he had escaped by a trick; and after various trips he had seized the occasion of the little ship which had just arrived to make his way happily to me.

I could not show enough gratitude to so generous and constant a friend. I took him to my house. I made him master of all I possessed. I told him everything that had happened to me since I left France, and, to give him a joy he was not expecting, I declared to him that the seeds of virtue, which he had once sown in my heart, were beginning to bring forth fruits with which he was going to be satisfied. He affirmed that so welcome an assurance repaid him for all the fatigues of his voyage.

We spent two months together in New Orleans, awaiting the arrival of ships from France, and, having at last put to sea, we landed two weeks ago at Le Havre. I wrote to my family on arriving. I learned, by my elder brother's reply, the sad news of my father's death,[17] to which I fear, with only too much reason, my wildness may have contributed. The wind being favorable for Calais, I embarked immediately, intending to go to the house of a gentleman who is a relative of mine, a few leagues from the town, where my brother writes that he is to await my arrival.

[17] In the 1731 edition, this sentence ends here.

SIGNET CLASSICS

and SIGNET Books by French authors

ADOLPHE AND THE RED NOTEBOOK *by Benjamin Constant*

By the close friend of Mme. de Stael, this 18th century French novel is the story of a young man's passion for a woman with whom he can never be happy. Introduction by Harold Nicolson.
(#CD1—50¢)

CANDIDE, ZADIG, AND SELECTED STORIES *by Voltaire*

In this fine collection of shorter works, the master of social commentary employs his ruthless wit to dissect science and spiritual faith, ethics and legal systems, love and human vanity. Newly translated, with an Introduction by Donald Frame.
(#CD35—50¢)

NIGHT FLIGHT *by Antoine de St.-Exupéry*

A novel of beauty and power about the intrepid flyers of the early, heroic age of aviation. Newly translated by Stuart Gilbert, Foreword by André Gide. (#CD46—50¢)

THE DEATH OF A NOBODY *by Jules Romains*

This noted modern classic, by a novelist considered "the French Dos Passos," tells how the memory of an unimportant nobody survives in the minds of all who knew him. Newly translated by Desmond MacCarthy and Sidney Waterlow, with an Afterword by Maurice Natanson. (#CD54—50¢)

CHERI AND THE LAST OF CHERI *by Colette*

Two vivacious and worldly-wise novels about an impetuous, handsome and pleasure-bent young man who takes whatever he wants from the many women in his life. (#D1761—50¢)

GIGI AND JULIE DE CARNEILHAN *by Colette*

A delightful novel of a wilful young girl who plays the game of love more shrewdly than her worldly aunt and grandmother.
(#S1525—35¢)

MOULIN ROUGE *by Pierre La Mure*

The colorful true-life story of Toulouse-Lautrec, painter and tragic lover of Paris' most exciting women. (#D1574—50¢)

TO OUR READERS

We welcome your request for our free catalog of SIGNET and MENTOR books. If your dealer does not have the books you want, you may order them by mail, enclosing the list price plus 5¢ a copy to cover mailing. The New American Library of World Literature, Inc., P. O. Box 2310, Grand Central Station, New York 17, N. Y.